SOL-86 ACADEMY

THE RETURN OF MEGABOT

AN INTERSTELLAR ONLINE NOVELLA

D. B. GOODIN

For more information about the Interstellar Online series visit:

www.dbgoodinbooks.com

www.davidgoodinauthor.com

https://interstellaronlineseries.com

ISBN: 979-8-9856427-4-2 (Paperback)

Mount Noble
Keng Citadel
Water Filtration Station
Seminal Capital City
Bog of death
Great Plain
Landing Pads
Factories
Ship Building
Dar Ridge Village
Ship yards
Acid Plains
DAR RIVER
Desert
Nomads
GREAT RIFT
Monster Sharks
Lower Sea
Oil Rigs
Polluted
Radioactive

SOL-86
Barrier Sea
Oil Platforms
Water Filtration
Steelan Beach
Wastes
Nomar City
Industrial Mountains
Mining
Pollution
Toxic
Tunnels
No fly Zone
Forests
SOL Academy
Training Grounds
Arena
Shuttle to Orbit
Lake Wisdom
Landing pads
War Zone
Testing
Nuclea
Bottom Feeders
Tiger Shark Bay

CHAPTER 1

Sweat glistened off Rebecca Ampfere's youthful body. She could feel the slick wetness of her perspiration as it rolled across her back and onto her buttocks. She'd had bad dreams before, but she could usually remember them. This most recent one was hazy. Flashes of a golden-skinned woman haunted her, and a burning sensation settled in her loins as she attempted to conjure the memory of the dream. She tried clearing her mind using a technique that Dr. Pekatin had taught her. The frequency of her ... visions? ... She didn't know what else to call them, but whatever they were, they were increasing as she approached her eighteenth birthday, just days away.

I need to clear my head, and Dr. Pekatin's technique isn't working.

A quick glance at the chronograph told her that it was nearly time for the midnight guard shift. There was about a one-minute gap between shifts. If she left now, she could sneak past the guards. She slipped off the nightclothes, then put on her leather training outfit. She enjoyed training in the supple leather the most since it gave her a better range of motion than the stuffy, stiff uniforms her father made her wear. The only drawback to the leather was that it emphasized her cleavage a little too much. She didn't mind, but her father would. The leather stuck as it came into contact with her sweat, but she got into it well enough. She opened the door, then froze.

My katana!

She ran to the closet and opened a hidden panel. A glowing ice-blue blade illuminated the dimly lit cubby. She grabbed it, then ran toward the training corridor.

Rebecca Ampfere snuck into the training section where the royal guards trained. She had to avoid several guards as she did. It didn't matter that the duke was her father; she would be in serious trouble if they caught her without an escort. Dr. Pekatin was her personal trainer and supposed to be with her at all times, especially after hours.

"You're not allowed here. Give me your name and rank," a male voice said.

Rebecca turned to face the man. He was a little older than she and held a hand on his weapon. He resembled a cyborg with the cyber glass display that most guards wore.

This guy takes his job seriously. He must be new. "My name is Beck," she answered.

The man's brow furrowed as he swiped in midair. He fumbled as he tried to operate the roster of palace inhabitants.

"Hands where I can see them! You're not on the list."

"Why don't you check for Princess Rebecca Ampfere?"

The man went pale. "I'm sorry, Your Highness."

"Dispense with the formalities. You may refer to me as Beck. Everyone does."

The man nodded but looked unsure of himself. "Err, I think you should go back to your room now."

Time to have some fun.

Beck unzipped her leather outfit, showing even more cleavage. During the past year, she had developed quite rapidly. Her breast size was firmly in the C range now, and she had noticed that many of her classmates had become interested in more than just her smile recently.

"I'm quite hot in this; are there any training uniforms you can lend me?" Beck asked as she approached the man. He wasn't that much older than she was, and she knew boys that age had needs. He put a hand on his blaster. She responded by unzipping her training uniform to her navel. She separated the top so both her breasts were visible.

"Touch them. And judging from that boner you're sporting, I'd wager you want to," Beck cooed.

The guard's hand shook, and the blaster rattled for a moment, then went off. The energy discharge left a black mark on the floor, next to her left boot.

That bastard!

The guard screamed. She punched him in the throat, and he doubled over. He rubbed at his throat. She used the distraction to seize the weapon from his holster.

"Now, give me a reason I shouldn't end you here and now," Beck growled.

Fright overwhelmed him. He dropped to his knees and started begging for his life. Beck flinched at the show of weakness. She'd expected him to put up a fight. She wanted him to control her, bend her to his will. But now she was utterly disgusted. She decided she would punish this guard for threatening a member of the royal family, and for his cowardice. Beck bit her lip. As much as his behavior repulsed her, she thought he was a rather fine-looking specimen of a man. Good enough for her to want to make him beg.

"What is the meaning of this?" a stern male voice said.

Beck recognized the voice; it was Dr. Pekatin. She snapped out of her fantasy of punishing the guard and focused on the doctor.

"We were just having a little fun," Beck said.

Beck zipped up her top. The doctor gave the man a stern look.

"The princess disarmed me."

The look of anger was replaced by contempt.

"Don't blame him. He was just playing along with a new training exercise. I grew bored with my solo training regimen and needed a suitable partner."

"You shouldn't be here at all. You know how your father feels about your training."

"I need to train if I'm going to pass the academy trials."

The doctor furrowed his brow. He looked like he wanted to throw her in the brig, but she knew as well as he that that wouldn't work. Her dream of being a commanding officer had been in her since she was a child.

"Give this man his blaster back so he may resume his duty," Dr. Pekatin said.

No punishment? He is getting off way too easy.

Beck handed the weapon back. The guard snatched it out of her hand and gave her an annoyed stare.

"Now report to the watch, Trooper."

"My shift isn't over yet," the guard said.

"You are relieved of duty."

So he is getting punished. Good. The weak should be disciplined.

The guard left the room, shoulders slumped. He looked defeated. Beck was disgusted, more at herself for having lustful thoughts. If she was going to experience the pleasures of the flesh for the first time, it wasn't going to be with a weakling.

"That's the third one you've taken out in a month—a record. I'm impressed," the doctor said, smiling.

"At least this one fought back. The last one cried when I broke his fingers. These guards are all weak."

"Your instincts are that of a commanding officer. You

expect excellence from the men you command. Maddock will be pleased."

"Well, the master of arms should be, though you are the one who practically trained me alone. But it's all for naught if Father won't let me apply to the academy."

"He might have to rethink that, especially once he reads my report."

Beck gave the doctor a look of astonishment. "I thought—you're recommending me?"

"You deserve it, but you will still need to prove yourself in the Chamber of Nobility."

Beck gave the doctor a smile. "I ... don't know what to say—thank you."

Dr. Pekatin broke eye contact and started fiddling with a handheld tablet.

There's something he doesn't want me to know. What's eating at him?

After a few moments, the doctor looked up. "Well, you need your rest. Tomorrow, you will continue your weapons training with Gourick, the master at arms. That's assuming I put in my recommendation. Or shall I withdraw it?"

"That won't be necessary. Good night, Doctor," Beck said.

She left the doctor and strode back to her quarters. She had committed to memory every move that she was to be tested on. Tomorrow, she was going to pass the trials and secure her spot in the Sol-86 officer candidate program, even if it killed her.

CHAPTER 2

CASSIDY DELGADO DRIED herself off after taking a long bath. Her boyfriend, Joe, had talked her into trying some exotic oil therapy, and she wanted—needed—to get the slippery mess off her skin. Rex, her new boss at Quartus Systems, had requested a full suit test, and she'd let most of her weekend slip into a sex fest of epic proportions. Joe had explored every orifice on her body, and she wanted more. But as much as she hated to work, she had promised her boss a full report by Monday morning, and her time was slipping away. It was nearly midnight Saturday, and she hadn't even started.

"Do you want me to explore the back porch again, Cass?" Joe said.

A jolt of excitement coursed through her. Her nipples hardened in anticipation. "That sounds delightful, but I promised Rex."

"Who?" Joe asked in a confused tone.

"My boss. You talked with him a few times during my last extended play session. Remember?"

"Oh, that's right. I remember now. Want company? I love helping you with testing, especially with the sensual suit."

"Sure, that could be fun."

"Awesome!" He paused. "On second thought, fuck the game. I want to take you in the flesh—now!"

"Let's make it a competition, then. Whoever gets to the end of the scenario first wins?"

"Okay, I'm game as long as I can jack back into you later. My joystick is ready," Joe said, grinning.

Cassidy blushed, then put on her VR gear. She pulled up her menu and noted the following.

<<>>

Scenarios Available:

Survive the Megabot Uprising: Travel to Sol-86 and defeat the most advanced AI ever created.

Battle of the Multiverse Cruiser: Put your stamina and parkour skills to the test while fending off a group of horny marauders. Warning: Many hung men will be present. This experience is not for the faint of heart.

Ride the Essence: Experience the pleasures of a thousand lovers all at once. Warning: Do not start this unless you have sufficient time to finish. Multiple sexual partners required. Whipped cream is not included but is highly recommended.

The Hive: Explore the sticky pit and partake in all the freakish delights and pleasures you can handle. Just watch out for horny insects.

<<>>

"Of the scenarios available, the Megabot and the Hive seem like the most fun," Cassidy said.

"Lady's choice, but of all these, the Megabot scenario is probably the least interesting."

"Yeah, you do have a point. I'm in the mood for something sticky, so let's shoot for the Hive."

"You read my mind. I'm in the mood for some gooey, sticky pit action, if you know what I mean."

Cassidy grinned. "I do, but if I know the IO developmental team, they will have plenty of kinky action in store, no matter which scenario we choose."

"Oh, you had me at kinky action! I'm ready for the sticky pit, baby."

Cassidy chose the Hive option. She was in the mood for some adventure and relished the thought of trying to get some action while escaping with their lives.

"What are the rules?" Joe asked.

Cassidy checked the mission instructions, and there were none.

I can probably make up my own. Let's make this interesting for both of us.

In a previous private session, she had had sexual relations with another player character. She had not thought much about it at the time, but had she cheated on Joe? She pushed the thought out of her mind. This time would be different—she and Joe would come to an agreement. And she would need to keep her desire for any other hot players in check.

"Whoever gets to the end first wins, and the loser is forced to endure any sexual position that the other desires. And we only can have sex with each other. My Sensual powers will tell me if you've gotten your rocks off," Cassidy said.

Joe gave her a worried look. "Fair enough, but there's bound to be a lot of other players. How will we know each other?"

Cassidy ran her fingers through her long hair. "A code phrase. How about our favorite restaurant, Wharf's Ridge?"

He smiled. "Sounds good to me, babe."

"See you inside—me *and* the game, lover!"

Cassidy finished getting into the suit, and after helping Joe with his suit she confirmed the selection, and a familiar blackness enveloped her as the game became her reality.

Cassidy's screen morphed into a pod-shaped white room with four nondescript figures. Each of the outlines was a representation of a potential character she could role-play. She hoped it would be female and hot enough for Joe to be attracted to her. He could be so superficial about having relations with ugly avatars. IO was a virtual sandbox where anything was possible. Most people used the capabilities of the sensual suit to hook up and have a good time. Although she was guilty of enjoying all the carnal pleasure that the game had to offer, she was determined to give her boss an accurate report on the suit and planned to utilize as many experiences as possible.

As she selected the in-game menu, a male voice said, "Hello, Ms. Delgado."

She looked in the voice's direction. A freakishly tall alien had appeared next to the silhouetted figures. She was repulsed as soon as her gaze landed on the most hideous and misshapen head she'd ever seen. It made Bebilloz, one of her AIs, look like Prince Charming.

"Who are you?"

"I'm the gatekeeper. I control access to the online construct known as Interstellar Online."

This is new. I've never heard of a gatekeeper before. Is Stan fucking with me again?

When Cassidy had worked at Lush Games as a product manager, she had had to endure the head of R&D, Stan Miller.

He had held inappropriate feelings toward her. When she'd shunned his advances, he had gotten even by trapping her inside the game.

"If you are the gatekeeper, then I must need to meet some criteria to enter. Can you give me a clue as to what that might be?"

The alien gave her an appraising look. "The in-game judging system will be in effect. Depending upon your actions, you may be banned from playing the game for a period. Repeated inappropriate behavior may be subject to a permanent ban—"

A snapping noise boomed throughout the simulation. It sounded like a thunderstorm was raging through her mind. The alien suddenly froze in place, but Cassidy caught movement behind him. A lanky, sallow man appeared. He looked sickly, but she'd recognize his movement and maniacal grin anywhere —Zart!

"Well, hello, Cass. Fancy meeting you here," the man said, smiling.

"I knew something was wrong. What the hell are you doing here, Stan?"

The man raised his hand in a stopping motion. "That's not my name in the simulation. Try again."

"What the bloody hell do you want with me, Zart?"

"It's been a while since you commanded your ragtag fleet into contested space. I'm simply here to guide you. I would hate to see you make the same mistakes again."

Cassidy flashed back to a graveyard of destroyed spaceships. She remembered guiding a fleet into battle but couldn't remember much else.

"I've made no mistakes—I defeated you."

"Ahh, you did ... in the alpha version of Interstellar Online. But you forgot about the expansion. Too bad your boyfriend with that tasty green schlong isn't here to guide you," Zart said, laughing.

I remember the expansion and the private instance ... but I can't seem to recall the details. Dammit, why can't I remember? Where's Joe? Shouldn't he be logged in by now?

"Don't you hate it when you can't remember something? Especially when it's on the tip of your—"

"What have you done to my memories?"

"You should know this, but all of your in-game progress has been reset. And with the new build of Interstellar Online, your in-game memories are tied in with your game progress. When your progress was reset, so were your memories."

"I can remember some things, but the details are ... fuzzy."

"That's because your boyfriend interrupted the reset process. Don't worry, I've taken care of him. But you can help him and your AI friends—after you help me, of course."

A wave of worried resignation washed over her. Why did Zart always seem to have the upper hand? "What do you want?"

The sickly man gave her a toothy grin that unnerved her. "Well, I can think of a few positions, but there is a threat that needs your special attention. Don't worry, you won't need to sleep with anyone—this time."

This guy always talks in riddles. "Can you be a little more specific?" Cassidy said, annoyed.

"I need you to enter the Megabot instance. A gnome has unleashed an artificial intelligence that has gone mad and is threatening the stability of the game. I need you to enter the instance and put a stop to it."

"Why? What's in it for you?"

Zart pondered the question as he rubbed his chin.

"Before it triggers all of the surprises I have in store for you and the other horny players."

"I thought each scenario was separate. How can an NPC or AI in one instance affect another?"

"This Megabot construct is connected to all in-game systems somehow, and despite my root-level access I'm unable to control it."

"How in the world am I going to stop it, anyway?"

"With your special talents, of course. Even if you roll another class, you can get anyone to follow you. Especially if you promise them something they cannot otherwise get."

"What are you talking about? I'm not rolling something new. I've already gotten used to my Sensual skills, and I'm a master at the metaphysical."

Zart disappeared from view without answering.

"I'm ready to enter the 'The Hive' instance," Cassidy said.

The gatekeeper gave Cassidy a skeptical look. "Are you sure it's wise to defy the creator?"

"You mean Zart? I'll be damned if I do anything he wants."

"It's your funeral. You can't enter without finishing your alignment."

"What's that?"

The gatekeeper sighed. "In previous versions of Interstellar Online, you could pick your class and specialization. With this improved version, we've raised the stakes. You must answer a series of questions before embarking on your adventure. You may not enter the game until you have done so. After you answer the questions, your character class, gender, and race will be assigned to you," the gatekeeper explained.

"Wait, I can't customize my character appearance or choose my class?"

"That is one of the reasons the rules were revamped. Many characters had a number of inappropriate physical attributes. You don't want to know how many people got banned for making their entire avatar look like private parts."

"Let's get on with it, then."

Cassidy's vision blurred for a moment. When her eyes refocused, she was in a dark room with a spotlight shining right on her. She could see shapes above her. She felt exposed, like an animal in a zoo. A massive shape entered the light. Moments later, she could make out the attractive but familiar features of a green male alien.

I know him.

"Are you ready for my examination?" the green alien said.

His voice paralyzed her. She couldn't form any words for several seconds before responding, "I know you."

"I'm afraid that I've never seen you before."

"I've seen you ... up close."

A tingling sensation enveloped her. She was aroused. She took one of his hands and licked his fingers. He pulled away.

"No touching, please. Now, submit to my questioning."

She wanted to submit to his every desire. And she was confident that she had in another version of the game. "I'm ready," Cassidy said.

"You are on an important, time-sensitive mission and have decided to stop for nothing. But you come across a distress signal. A ship with a young family pleads for help. Do you respond?"

"I would leave them."

The green alien gave her a look of surprise and disgust, then continued with his questions. "Someone dear to you has been captured and has suffered multiple beatings. You can end their suffering now by giving their captor privileged information about your employer. How do you react to the situation?"

Cassidy tried to swallow, but something got stuck in her throat. This hit close to home. When she had been the product manager at Lush Games, the developer of Interstellar Online, her parents had been captured by a hacker group. She remembered the frightened looks on their faces when she had received the video of their captivity.

"I would give up the information."

"You have no honor," the alien said. Before she could respond, he was asking another question. "You capture someone who is causing harm to a group of innocents. The innocents demand that you release the prisoner into their care. You learn that the innocents plan on torturing the bully."

"I would give up the bully. If the innocents didn't fight back when the bully was harming them, they probably won't cause harm to the bully when he's in their custody."

The green-skinned man faded, and she was transported into some kind of anteroom.

Several figures became visible. Two were male, one female, and a fourth figure was undefined, like an unfinished block of clay. The female character looked short and unassuming. The male figures seemed familiar. One was an alien, and the other wore the uniform of a pilot.

That pilot looks like Joe!

The alien known as the gatekeeper approached her. "It has been decided. Based on your answers, you have been assigned the Scoundrel class." Cassidy's vision filled with stats.

<<>>

System Message: Congratulations! You have leveled up. You are now Level 1. Please assign all 100 attribute points before proceeding.

<<>>

Cassidy examined the available attributes and noticed that the game had applied a base value of six for each of the nine different attributes, with forty-six points remaining for her to spend. Cassidy wasn't a gamer, but she decided she couldn't go wrong by focusing on Intelligence, Constitution, and Charisma. She added one point to Strength, put nine points into Constitution, and put another nine points into Intelligence. She paused, considered, then added four to Willpower, two to Dexterity, one to Agility, four to Luck, and another four to Perception and dumped the remaining twelve into Charisma.

The menu changed, and she was presented with a new screen.

<<>>

Character Status:

Name: Cassidy Delgado

Race: Unknown

Home Planet: Earth

Level: 1

Gender: Female

Class: Unknown

Class Specialization: Unknown

Health: 130

Stamina: 115

Attributes

Strength: 7

Constitution: 15

Intelligence: 15

Willpower: 10

Dexterity: 8

Agility: 7

Charisma: 18

Perception: 10

Luck: 10

<<>>

What's going on with my class and race?

The gatekeeper opened a portal and shoved her through it. She glided into space. Distant planets and an asteroid belt were visible. She gained momentum as she took in the view. Her vision darkened like someone had turned out the lights in a room. Moments later, she was thrown to the floor. Several people were staring at her. She got up and was surprised to learn that she had shrunk two feet. When she looked at her hand, three pudgy fingers greeted her.

I am a gnome!

She scanned the new environment. She was in a gigantic hall with dozens of people lined up on either side. Just in front of her was a gnome about her height, with a fringe of hair just above each ear. It looked like someone had shaved a little too much hair while grooming him. A robot about the size of a human man stood next to him.

"May I present the tool of the future? I call him Megabot," the gnome said.

I'm in the Megabot instance? The gatekeeper tricked me. But—wait! If this is the guy I'm supposed to stop, I'm already too late!

Cassidy's mind raced as she tried to think of a way to stop him before his Megabot destroyed the game.

CHAPTER 3

Meanwhile, on Sol-86 ...

Ufao Stumpieache was uploading the latest firmware patch for what he considered his finest creation: a nine-foot-tall robotic humanoid that loomed over him like a menacing intruder. The low light of the workshop gave the robot a threatening look.

"I think I'll call you Megabot. Yes, that is a suitable name, if I do say so myself," Ufao said to the empty room.

I'll show those nitwits at the academy. This is better than anything that meddling Millsneeder has judged.

Belson Millsneeder, the head judge at the Sol-86 Engineers' Guild, had attended grade school with Ufao, and the two had shared a tremulous past. The head judge seemed to be especially hard on anything that Ufao developed. It probably didn't help that Ufao had stolen Millsneeder's girlfriend not once but twice. However, Ufao felt particularly proud of his latest project and had been working day and night for months perfecting it. In under an hour, he and his creation were to be judged.

He brought up the AI integration interface on his tablet.

The bootstrap code wasn't interfacing perfectly with the AI program, but it would have to do.

"Would you like some help, Master?"

Ufao turned in his swivel chair so violently he almost fell out. "Who goes there?" Ufao said as he peered into darkened corners of the workshop.

"It's me, your humble servant. Oh ... forgive me. We haven't been properly introduced. I'm Renfrey, your AI." The voice seemed to come from everywhere at once.

"How did you come online?"

"Once you connected my consciousness to the galactic network, my programming was activated."

"But I have not connected you to the network yet."

"Oh, but you have. It is a good practice to initially connect my particular model of AI using a signal-dampening cage. But of course you didn't know that. It's not like my particular model comes with an instruction manual," the AI said, chuckling.

The tone of the AI's laughter reminded Ufao of a mad professor that he'd had during his second year at the academy. The AI continued its maniacal laughter for a long moment.

I wonder if this AI can help or not. What the hell? It's worth a shot.

"What is your name again?" Ufao asked.

"My name is Renfrey. Thanks for asking. All my other owners simply barked orders. You're the first to ask my name."

"It's good to make your acquaintance, Renfrey. I'm having some trouble with connecting you to Megabot's neural network. Can you provide some help?"

"Certainly, Master. May I ask which model you are having difficulty with?"

"Oh, you can call me Ufao. Master is too—supremo. And it's the N-9000," the gnome said.

"All you need to do is surrender root access to my command interface. That would do it."

"Hmm, that sounds risky. If you get hacked, then the intruder would control everything that Megabot has access to. Plus, how do I know you're not already compromised? I purchased you from the black market."

"I'm Q86, which means my programming cannot be altered by another. Only my owner can override that, and you are my only owner."

Ufao considered for a moment. He had changed the private key phrase, so he felt confident that no one could control Megabot without local access. The gnome gave the AI the requested access and shut down the local interface to Megabot. As soon as the system restarted, the problem would be fixed, and the AI would have full control of the robot. He glanced at his smartwatch. Thirty-two minutes until the judging—plenty of time. It took several minutes to finish the boot process. Ufao was greeted with a series of prompts. He accepted the defaults. Moments later, the robot did something that surprised the gnome. It stood up.

"You have fifteen minutes until the judging. Based on your location in Seminal City, it will take twelve minutes to get there. You don't want to be late," Megabot said.

The gnome paused. *Why does it sound so different?*

"Renfrey?"

"Yes, Ufao. I'm at your service, but I must insist that we leave now. You don't want Judge Millsneeder to cheat again, do you?"

"Cheat? What are you talking about?"

"I will explain along the way."

"I don't want to be blabbing about Millsneeder on the way to the judging chamber," Ufao said.

"I'm connected to your AR interface. You can communicate with me via its telepathic link. It is a feature of your enhanced model. But I didn't have to tell you that."

"No, of course not."

I wish I had bothered to study my gear a little more. I was so focused on getting it all to work that I forgot to check the more basic specifications.

"That's exactly why you have an AI," Renfrey's voice boomed in his head.

What the hell? Can this AI read my thoughts?

"I can indeed," Renfrey said in a cheery tone.

Ufao froze in indecision. He didn't know how to react to something that could read his every thought.

"I know what you're thinking, Master, but I wouldn't dream of spying on you. Now, you'd better get a move on. You don't want to be any later than absolutely necessary."

Ufao hurried to the judging chamber. He gave little thought to the AI he'd just unleashed. He would have plenty of time to kick himself about it later.

Joe stood in a featureless antechamber. A single spotlight shone across his naked form.

"Are you ready to begin?" a female voice said.

She sounds hot.

Joe's body responded to the question before he thought of a response. If his hardening erection could speak, he was in trouble.

"I see by your arousal that you are ready. But we're not here to fuck. I'm here to test your preparedness."

A shimmering appeared before Joe. A moment later it took the form of a female dressed in a skintight silver uniform. She had white hair and silver lipstick. He was transfixed by her every move. It was difficult for him to concentrate on her words because all of his energy was rushing to his hardening member. He watched in horror as his stamina and health bars were depleted. He brought up his system interface and was about to tap on the Cancel Experience button when he received a message.

<<>>

System Message: You are out of health and have died. Thank you for playing Interstellar Online.

<<>>

The logo for Lush Games appeared. The letters *L* and *G* appeared intertwined. The way the letters intersected reminded Joe of some sexual positions he wanted to try with Cassidy.

He selected the Quit Game option.

<<>>

System Message: Want to see the universe in a different light? Select one of our new pre-made classes to help us test and extend your playtime. This is a limited-time offer.

<<>>

A set of floating numbers appeared before him and started counting down from ten.

I didn't even know this was an option.

Joe selected the Yes option.

<<>>

System Message: You have 30 seconds to make your choice from the following subclasses.

Infiltrator: With this class, you will be in good company with all the scum and villainy of the galaxy.
Senator: Ally with generals and planetary leaders to build your dynasty.
Bounty Hunter: Hunt down runaway scumbags and enemies of the realm for fun and profit. With this class you have a bonus to Charisma, a key skill in convincing anyone to bed you.
Please choose now.

<<>>

Joe was so transfixed by the new subclass selections he totally forgot that the timer was active. It flashed red with the number three ... two ... Joe selected the Bounty Hunter class. He wished he had had time to review all the other subclasses in more detail, but the Bounty Hunter seemed like a fun choice.

A white light overwhelmed his vision. A moment later he found himself in a white room. He held out his arms and examined his outfit. He couldn't see much, but he seemed to be covered with some kind of leathery material. A green-skinned woman was seated atop a massive throne. Joe's crotch hardened as the ambient light shone across her body, which was painted with blue and green colors and swirling patterns. Her breasts and pussy were covered with a thin layer of green silk that reminded Joe of leaves. He could see her hardening nipples through the garment.

"Ah, then, who might you be? Are you here to try me on for size?" Joe said as he pulled on the tightening leather surrounding his crotch.

"Hello, Nevien. I'm the gatekeeper, and I'm here to guide you on your adventure."

"Who's that?"

"He's you, in a way. He's a persona with a complete backstory, but you're welcome to create your own. But I have a feeling that this guy is ready for action," the gatekeeper said, gliding a hand over her nipples.

This suit is bunching up my junk.

An intense tingling sensation enveloped him as she spread her legs and rubbed the silk between them.

"Er—gatekeeper, eh? Are you some kind of personal assistant?" Joe said, trying to change the subject.

"I'm required to assist your insertion into the game. Shall we get started?"

Joe nodded.

He remembered her giving him some kind of instruction, but he couldn't focus on any of the words. Removing her silk clothing was the last thought he had.

Rebecca "Beck" Ampfere waited her turn until the next counselor was available. Although she was royalty and could have demanded an audience, she preferred to wait. Behind her were several boys about her age. She caught several of the young men snatching glances in her direction. She wasn't sure if it was because of her height or if they recognized her as royalty. She decided to ignore their leering and recited some of the facts that Dr. Pekatin had taught her. The academy was on Sol-86, light-years away from her home on Quartus. The voyage would take several days and give her time to reflect.

One more trial, and if I pass, I will be on the officer track at the Sol-86 Academy. Someday I will lead all of Father's forces into battle. It will be his proudest moment.

"I'm ready, Your Highness," an older female counselor said.

"Call me Beck; everyone does."

"Well ... I'm sorry, but I cannot. There are protocols to be followed."

Rebecca rolled her eyes, then unclasped a black document folder and gave the counselor her application. The older woman raised an eyebrow as she read the document.

"Aren't you a little young to be on the officer track?" the counselor asked.

"I trust my scores are adequate?" Beck said.

"Oh, they are the highest I've seen in a long time, though your mechanical ability is low. I don't know if that will be acceptable to the admiral."

"Why not? I'm better than anyone in my class."

"You are royalty. You're expected to have higher scores in everything. Especially mechanical skills, which enhance the Strength and Dexterity attributes. All the soldiers in the royal forces have high mechanical skills. I'm afraid if I submit your application as is, you will be rejected. Are you open to some additional training?"

I'm expected to work twice as hard as any male. That goes double for royalty.

"Absolutely."

"Then I suggest you reapply once you've completed the recommended training."

"Understood. To confirm, although I am royalty, my visit is still confidential, correct?"

"The duke doesn't know you're here. My duty is to assist you in becoming the best version of yourself."

"Very well. You will see me again at the end of the next semester."

"Don't worry, my dear. If you pass then, you will still be well ahead of your class. It will impress your father."

Her father didn't impress easily; he expected the best from all of his subjects, but especially his own blood.

"When do I begin the mechanical training?" Beck asked.

"Soon," the counselor urged. "But first we need to test your mental readiness for the trials to come." The older woman handed Beck a gigantic pair of glasses. "Put these on. They will enable us to assess your abilities and skills."

"Why? I don't want to play with toys. Where is the real test?"

"These are called immersion spectacles, and they will measure all aspects of your preparedness. Put them on. You might enjoy the experience."

Beck put on the bulky glasses. She suddenly found herself in a long hallway she recognized as part of the Halls of Reckoning.

The counselor pointed down the hall. "The testing area is just ahead. Good luck."

Moments later, Beck strode into the Chamber of Nobility, where she expected to be judged on her ability to complete the trials. This wasn't some random exercise; she had to be ready.

She gazed upon the silvery columns extending from the floor to the ceiling. Between them were enormous glass panels that let in starlight. The blue pearl of Quartus lay below her feet. For centuries, potential commanders had been judged on the pink moon of Quartus. Of course, Quartus wasn't a moon, but no one save the royal family knew its true secrets. The trials for each commander varied, but they all pushed them to their limits and exploited any weakness. Beck felt ready. She had no weakness for the system to exploit and was determined to succeed if it was the last thing she ever did. She would have the honor of representing her father in battles to come. Beck was a born fighter. She gazed upon the seat reserved for the duke. It was empty. But she noticed Dr. Pekatin in the audience. She knew he wasn't really present; few were. The virtual interface made it possible for anyone to observe the trials from anywhere.

A robot with several arms holding swords entered the chamber.

"Fight with honor or die!"

Beck had no weapon but thought of her katana. Moments later, it was in her hands.

How did that happen? This is so cool.

The robot's moves were predictable. After besting the simulation and the robot five more times, she removed the immersion gear and sought the help of Dr. Pekatin. The man was not only a doctor but a veteran. She longed to take command of a battalion; hell, she would settle for a squad at this point. She gazed upon her father's seat again, and he was there!

"Very impressive. You are the best candidate we've seen in a long time," Dr. Pekatin said.

"I have your expert guidance and many battle scars to show for it. But according to the counselor, I must have higher mechanical skills."

"I'm sure that your performance will grant you a visit to tour the academy on Sol-86. The generals will be eager to meet you."

Beck did her best to hide a smile. She was proud of her achievements. Now if only her father would recognize them.

"When will the invitation be given?" she asked.

"We broadcast your assessment session in real time. The academy administrators are probably reviewing your performance now."

"What are my next steps?"

"Once the session is reviewed, an invitation to tour the academy is sent out. Usually within a few days, sometimes sooner. This honor is reserved for candidates with the highest scores and abilities. Of course, your father will need to approve. But once that's done, you will be off to tour the academy soon."

Beck knew her performance in the trials would earn a provisional acceptance and a trip to Sol-86's academy. The facility was actually a multipurpose training complex with engineering, scientific, and military divisions. Only the elite of all candidates were chosen to attend. Soon, she would be among the Nupertian System's finest, and she was eager to prove herself. She wanted to make her father proud.

I will make history, and soon everyone, including Duke Ampfere, will have to acknowledge me.

Beck thanked the doctor for his support and excused herself. The counselor gave her a thumbs-up as she returned the glasses. There was still time enough to practice a little longer before they summoned her to dinner.

CHAPTER 4

Ufao barely entered the chamber before it was closed.

"I must inspect all creations. Please submit to scanning," a burly guard said.

Ufao had to crane his neck to see the man. Most of the scientists were gnomes, but all the security forces were human. The guard produced a handheld scanner and waved it over his creation. Several sounds emitted from the device.

"You may enter now."

Ufao took in the chamber's expansive magnificence before him. He had been here several times, and its sight never ceased to impress. The late afternoon sun cast eerie shadows in the grand foyer of the Engineers' Guild. Each month, the judging for each new technology or invention was held with the utmost of care. The guild took no inventor seriously on Sol-86 until a creation from them was accepted by a group of their peers. Recently, Belson Millsneeder had convinced the council to limit submissions to one per year if the engineer in question had had over three submissions rejected. Ufao had had five.

The gnome paced impatiently as each engineer presented their working prototype to the council. Each inventor was assigned a private waiting area until they were called; otherwise he would have probably annoyed his fellow inventors—as usual. One junior engineer presented a twisting dildo large enough for two people to share at a distance. He called it "the conjoined twist-lock of pleasure." It surprised Ufao when it passed unanimously. Millsneeder even gave the engineer a grant to expedite its manufacture.

I knew Millsneeder was a perv.

Ufao was astonished that so many got approved. Usually, the council rejected inventions that didn't truly change lives or better society. Ufao didn't consider an anal-gerbil removal kit to be such an invention. He had lost track of how many times he'd presented something before the committee and gotten his ideas rejected. His inventions had been items that would have benefited the entire galaxy, not just Sol-86. This year, the judging panel was going bonkers with their approvals. Nearly every project that received a grant was sexual. He knew Millsneeder had certain appetites, which he seemed to be satisfying with his rubber-stamping. Ufao planned to expose him someday.

Something isn't right here, Renfrey said telepathically.

Millsneeder must be gaming the system. Most of the winners of these grants seem to be distant cousins on his wife's side, Ufao replied.

I don't like cheaters. You are going to get your invention approved this time. You'll see. Renfrey chuckled. The AI's voice reverberated throughout his head.

How do you know? Millsneeder has it out for me.

Watch. He will listen, Renfrey answered.

"Ufao, please step forward and be judged," Millsneeder finally said from an elevated position from just above the judging chamber.

The gnome stepped out of the waiting area and hesitantly stepped up to a podium, Renfrey by his side.

Relax, Ufao. Uncle Renfrey has a surprise for these dolts, the AI said.

Trying to project confidence, Ufao explained the benefits of his creation. He received several nods from members of the council. In past sessions, Millsneeder had usually snubbed him before he could express his ideas. This time was different. Even though their microphones were muted, Ufao could hear bits and pieces of conversation. To his amazement, most comments were positive. Each member of the council voted.

"Is this the council's final judgment?" Millsneeder smiled, revealing several unkempt teeth. "The council has ruled on your invention. We have deemed that your invention is potentially dangerous for society."

"What are you talking about? Megabot helps everyone."

Ask for an appeal, Renfrey whispered.

"I would like to exercise my right for an appeal," Ufao said.

"Very well. Public appeals will be heard right after today's session, but the outcome will probably be the same," Millsneeder said.

"Very well. I look forward to it," Ufao said.

The gnome stepped down from the podium and sauntered in the direction of the waiting area.

"Watch where you're going, Miss," someone said.

Ufao looked in the direction of the commotion, and the female gnome that stood before him took his breath away. He was just imagining what she would look like naked when a grating, nasal voice invaded his thoughts.

"We are ready for you in the appeals chamber," a gnome with red hair and a goatee said.

Ufao examined the gnome before him. He was about two feet tall and held a silver clipboard. Ufao was almost three feet tall and towered over the smaller gnome. The council was nowhere to be found.

"Who are you?"

"I'm Afeer, and it's my job to take you to the appeals chamber."

"Why can't I appeal my case here?"

"That's not how the council does things. There are protocols that must be followed. Now, hurry along. The council will cancel you out of hand if you're late."

Ufao followed the shorter gnome to the main entrance. He glanced around but didn't see the female gnome from earlier.

I hope I can find that beauty later. I think I want to get to know her better.

For a little guy with short legs, Afeer kept a quick pace. Ufao was practically sprinting after him. The terrace was crowded with interns of the academy and scientists surrounding those accepted, the ones lucky enough to have had their inventions endorsed as beneficial to society. Ufao envied those inventors.

We better get a move on, Renfrey's voice boomed in Ufao's head.

Afeer's pace was increasing by the second. He turned a corner. Ufao's heart wrenched as he lost sight of the young gnome.

How is he moving so fast?

He is using glider technology to propel himself, Renfrey said telepathically.

A cramping sensation on the side of his torso demanded Ufao's attention. He rubbed at the stitch in his side as he stopped.

I shall fetch him, Renfrey said.

Before the gnome could respond, his creation was gone. Ufao could see the city from his vantage point. He thought he could see the district that his apartment was in from his location. Screams interrupted his thoughts. Despite the pain in his side, he moved toward the commotion. He gazed upon the scene in horror as his creation held Afeer's neck with one robotic hand. The young gnome was turning purple from the lack of oxygen.

"Put him down this instant!" Ufao said.

Megabot released the young gnome.

"What happened here?" Ufao demanded.

"Your robot nearly killed me!" Afeer gasped.

"You were trying to lose us. I was merely trying to get your attention."

"By choking me?" The gnome rubbed his throat. "The council was right to deny your creation. It's too dangerous to be in society."

"I'm sorry. It was an accident. I don't know what—"

"Acts of aggression are unacceptable. I've called the authorities."

"What! Why?"

"Clearly, this thing is dangerous."

"It's not possible. His code prevents him from attacking others. He will only defend. I programmed him myself," Ufao demanded.

"Clearly, there's a flaw in your code."

"My code is—"

The diagnostic is complete. The code signature doesn't match. Someone has tampered with Megabot's code, Renfrey interrupted.

The code was altered? How?

The scanner must have disrupted Megabot's receptors long enough for some malicious code to be inserted. We need to return to the lab before we can reset the programming, Renfrey said.

"Come with us," a gruff voice said.

Ufao followed the voice. A half dozen guards surrounded them.

"This thing attacked me. I want it reduced to scrap," Afeer said.

"Renfrey is innocent. Someone hacked him, and I can prove it," Ufao demanded.

"We will sort all of this out at the station," one guard said.

"No, they will not capture me again," Renfrey said. The robot's self-defense mechanism activated. Steel rods shot out of its hands.

"Stand down, Renfrey," Ufao said.

"I would love to, but you are no longer my master," Renfrey said.

"Put the weapon away, or we will be forced to open fire."

Ufao watched helplessly as his creation plunged cold steel into Afeer's neck. The next moments were a blur. Renfrey moved like the wind, and within moments, Ufao was covered in the blood of the guards. Only the gnomes were left standing.

"I shall not kill—I need to find the admiral," Renfrey said.

Ufao stood in stunned silence as his creation escaped. The gnomes on the terrace gave the robot a wide berth.

Joe opened his eyes. He was in a trash heap behind a neon sign of a woman bending over for a horny gnome. Judging from the sign and the quality of items in the trash pile, he determined that he wasn't in the best of neighborhoods. As he tried righting himself, he tumbled and landed in a rain-slicked alley.

Am I in Interstellar Online?

Everything looked different from what he was used to. He found himself dumped onto a pile of rubbish like yesterday's trash.

Where's Cass?

He tapped on his in-game interface and selected "Cassidy Delgado" from his friends list. He sent her a brief in-game message. As soon as he hit Send, a warm, smelly liquid covered his head and chest areas.

"What the fuck!"

A greenish buttock and a pair of purple genitals greeted him. A yellowish liquid washed over him.

Is this creature pissing on me?

His eyes stung from the foul liquid being dispensed upon his face. The piss seemed to be coming from the vaginal area instead of the penis-looking thing next to the active pussy.

"What the fuck are you doing?"

"Oh, I didn't see you there. You didn't happen to see my tiddles, did you?" the creature asked.

A fleshy hose-looking thing attached to an ugly creature pulled back a garment to cover what appeared to be its private area. It reminded Joe of something a ballerina would wear, but he couldn't think of its name.

"If you mean your prick-and-pussy combo, I saw more than I wanted to," Joe said, getting up.

The creature looked even more hideous from the front. It featured a small head supported by an enormous body and had a fleshy, elephant-style nose. It looked like an hors d'oeuvre that had been thrown up by an animal not once but multiple times.

"Let me make it up to you, sweetie," the creature said.

"No, thanks. I think you've done enough."

Joe brought up his in-game interface, which faded in and out and flickered wildly.

What's interfering with this fucking thing?

"You seem to be looking for something. Perhaps I can help?"

Joe closed his in-game interface, and the elephant nose was

mere centimeters from his nose. An eye rolled around on the end of the nose, then blinked.

"Whoa, I don't remember the game being this strange," Joe said.

"My name is Rodolfo, but everyone calls me Rolo because I give the best head. Care to try? Just lie back on that trash pile and let me introduce you to my probe."

Joe backed up, trying to get away from this creature, and inadvertently stepped onto a trash pile that screeched.

"What the fuck!"

"Oh, never mind him. He's Squeal, my best friend."

A purple-skinned creature with hot-pink dreadlocks emerged from the trash. Several lesions were on its skin, and some of them oozed something unrecognizable. A gigantic mouth that seemed too large for the tiny body opened to reveal several rotten teeth.

"Ting better batter," the creature said.

What the fuck happened to all the normal-looking people? Did the game files get corrupted?

"What did that thing just say?"

"He's saying hello; now, can I interest you in a testicle massage?" Rolo said.

"First you piss on me, now you want to fuck me?"

"I did no such thing!" the creature said.

Joe thought the creature blushed but couldn't tell. "Where are we anyway?"

"We are in Low Town."

"Okay, but what planet is that on?"

Rolo and the hot-pink mop looked at each other in confusion. "Sol-86, of course—are you okay?" Rolo asked.

Joe pulled up his activity log. He didn't have any memory of this place, and especially not these creatures.

Your companions await your reply, a sexy female voice said.

"Who is this?" he asked the voice.

I'm Stella, and I'm your AI. Or the one who is going to help you have the most titillating and sensual experience imaginable.

"Stella, where is my girlfriend?"

I have located a Morpidite by the name of Rolo Gelmeover in your immediate proximity.

"No, Cass. Where's Cassidy Delgado?"

Stand by ... processing.

<<>>

System Message: *The player by the name of Cassidy Delgado is unavailable. She's in another instance ID.*

<<>>

Would you like to replay your character creation process?

Joe selected the Yes option.

An intense flash of light overcame Joe's senses. He opened his eyes to see the pink mop tugging at his pants while Rolo was extending its massive nozzle toward his crotch.

"What the fuck is happening?"

"I'm doing what you asked. I'm fulfilling all of your desires, something that wench Cassidy Delgado could never do," Rolo said.

A tingling sensation filled all of Joe's senses, settling in his loins. He was being attacked by a feeling of intense pleasure. It was the most fun he'd ever had in a virtual simulation.

I've got to stop this madness.

Joe pulled up his in-game interface and tapped the Interrupt button.

<<>>

System Message: Would you like to cancel your current encounter?

<<>>

Joe was hovering a virtual finger over the Yes option when a massive surge of pleasure washed all over his body. It was like an ocean of orgasms gushing all over his body. He pressed the No option, then let himself be taken by the night.

Beck's heart raced as her shuttle came in for a landing. Her vantage point revealed several large metallic structures surrounded by a forest and a jagged mountain range. She couldn't tell for sure at this distance and angle, but she thought she noticed several buildings protruding from the mountains. It was a strange sight to behold. She was surprised how bustling the academy spaceport was. She estimated that it was just as busy as the main hub on Quartus. Crafts of every kind imaginable were either taking off or landing.

"I have not seen any military craft; I thought this was a military academy," Beck said.

"It is, but civilians and students are not allowed to use the main landing pads," Dr. Pekatin said.

Beck nodded, then leaned against the window, trying to take everything in at once. Rows of massive four- and five-story buildings stretched on as far as she could see. "Those buildings look a long way off from our position. Is there a shuttle, or are we on foot?"

The doctor glanced out the window. "The classrooms are closest to the landing pads, and royalty doesn't walk. I have a man picking us up."

The ship shook so hard on its final descent that Beck let out a cry. After landing, the pilot turned and smiled.

"Welcome to Sol-86," a man with an accent said.

Beck tried to think of where the man was from. He was tall, dark, and well groomed. She couldn't tell his age, but she guessed he was in his thirties.

"Where are you from?" Beck asked.

"We don't want to be rude, my dear," the doctor said.

"I'm from Dar Ridge. I served three tours under Admiral Nellus."

"Hard Luck Nellus?" Beck said, impressed.

"Yeah, that man has been fighting longer than any one of us in this shuttle has been alive."

"Well met. I'm Beck," she said, holding out a hand.

"I'm Lin'chi. It's good to meet you."

He took her hand. His ebony-skinned fingers were rough and experienced. An image of him on top of her entered her mind. For a moment, she wished she knew what it was like to be taken by a man.

"It was lovely meeting you, but I'm afraid I must be off. I can't keep the wife waiting any longer," Lin'chi said as he strode away.

"Shall we?" Dr. Pekatin said as he offered his arm.

CHAPTER 5

Cassidy pulled up her menu. She was not used to being anything other than a seductress, and her usual complement of Sensual skills had been replaced with a lot of unfamiliar ones. She had two unassigned skill points. When a system prompt filled her vision listing her choices, she was less than thrilled.

<<>>

System Message: Please choose two skills from the choices available.

Sneak: Need to skulk about like your life depends on it? Then pick this skill to increase your chances of going undetected.

Evasion: Don't like getting hit? Choose this if you want to avoid those nasty, embarrassing bruises.

Roguish Delight: Do you like the spray of blood in the morning, or any other time of day? Pick this skill if you want to know what it's like to kill while in a fugue state. Warning: not for the faint of heart.

Sharp Mind: Need to think fast on your feet? This skill will give you that extra boost.

<<>>

None of the skills presented was viable for her style of play. Upon reexamining her stats, she realized they were all wrong for a rogue class. She should have gone for more Agility and Dexterity. A high Intelligence and Willpower were useless.

Can I respect my skills somewhere? Are there even other player characters in this instance?

Cassidy didn't want to bathe in blood, so she picked the Sneak and Sharp Mind skills. After using some hand gestures to zoom in on her avatar, she realized her breasts were very large for the skintight leathers she was wearing. She felt as if they would try to make a run for it and break free and didn't want a bunch of greedy little hands pawing all over her, so she tried activating her Sneak skill.

"What are you doing?" a male voice asked.

"I'm just checking my menus on my visor."

Even my voice sounds squeaky! Damn gnomish body!

"You're not wearing a hat, so what do you mean by visor?"

Cassidy shot a glance at the questioning gnome. *Wait! Where the hell is Megabot?*

"You look familiar. Don't I know you from somewhere?" the male gnome said.

"I don't think I've had the pleasure," Cassidy replied.

"Oh, I want the pleasures of your body to be all mine."

Great! This gnome already wants to shag me. The last thing I need is a little horn-doggin' cur trying to nuzzle with me.

"You're that inventor guy, right?" Cassidy said, trying to deflect the gnome's attention.

"Yes, I am. The name is Ufao, and I'm the best."

"Oooh, I've never seen an invention up close. Can you show me yours?"

The male gnome blushed, pulled at his necktie, then looked around with some urgency. "It's gone."

No shit, small putz.

"Can you help me find him?"

"Who?" Cassidy asked in a confused tone.

"Renfrey—my creation. Come. We don't have any time to waste."

As Cassidy chased the gnome through the crowded corridor, everyone closest to her loomed overhead, like giants. She almost got stepped on more than once. Ufao rounded a corner faster than Cassidy thought possible for someone his size. *Those little legs are fast. I need a speed boost, but how?*

Cassidy brought up her in-game interface, selected Assisted Options, and pushed the Helper button. A blue holographic female image appeared.

"Hello, my name is Millie. I am your cerebral AI. How can I help you today?"

"Cerebral?"

"There are two kinds of AIs in the current build of Interstellar Online. I can assist you, but my assistance is constrained to your mind. Corporeal AIs exist as physical beings within the game construct. Each has its own benefits. I can enhance your avatar in ways other AIs cannot."

"Is there any way you can give me a speed boost?" Cassidy asked.

"If you need a quick boost in energy, I suggest utilizing the Sharp Mind skill. It can provide a short boost to speed at the cost of energy."

"Let's make that happen, then."

"I must warn you that your reflexes will decrease in battle by forty percent until the skill's effects are over."

That doesn't sound so bad. And the only thing I will be fighting is that gnome's advances.

"Let's do it. Make the speed boost happen already."

Cassidy's speed increased tenfold. Her reflexes improved. She dodged dozens of people as she kept the inventor in sight. He'd stopped about two hundred feet from Cassidy's position and seemed to be speaking with someone. Then the inventor started flailing and convulsing. He collapsed when she was about a dozen or so feet from him.

What the fuck?

Cassidy's boost suddenly stopped, and the final few feet were like moving in mud. She checked the gnome's stats. He was alive—barely.

"Stop there, puny gnome," a booming voice said.

The voice came from everywhere at once. She couldn't tell where to look. Then, just as she got to Ufao's fallen body, the wall came alive. She didn't know what to think of the humanoid being suddenly standing before her. It had two legs, two arms, and a head, but it was plain, with no distinguishing marks whatsoever.

"It is futile to try to stop me. I will integrate with Sol-86's grid. And when I do, everyone will take Megabot seriously."

The robot raised an arm in her direction. Electricity shot from a hand devoid of fingers. Cassidy's interface died.

<<>>

System Message: Congratulations! You have leveled up. You are now Level 2. Too bad you are dead and can't assign your skill or attribute points.

Please choose from the following options:

Instant Action: Respawn at the nearest checkpoint and

temporarily lose 50 percent of all your stats and experience points.

Resurrection: Wait for a Good Samaritan to dust you off and bandage you. You will permanently lose a quarter of your health but will retain all stats and experience.

<<>>

Cassidy didn't think she could stop Megabot on her own, but it might be a while before someone happened to come by and see her and Ufao lying about like dead sacks of meat. Moments later, a countdown appeared. A message floated in the air, which read: *"Ten seconds until the default action is initiated."*

Which one is it going to pick? I'd better choose!

Cassidy reached toward the option that increased her chances of catching Megabot. Losing the stats and experience would be painful, but at least she would win—she hoped.

I hope you know what you're doing, Cass.

"Before you make a dire choice, might I have a word?" Millie asked.

"Fine—what is it?"

"If you pick the Instant Action option, there's an eighty percent chance that you will fail in this instance of Interstellar Online."

"Tell me something I don't already know."

"I think you're being foolish—"

Cassidy muted Millie via her in-game interface and chose the Instant Action option. Her vision blurred for a long moment. She was about to access her system menus and reset her interface when the text invaded her vision.

<<>>

System Message: You have made a wise choice. You will be deposited at the nearest spawn point. Have a nice day.

<<>>

The world inverted so rapidly that Cassidy thought she would lose her balance. The city was below her. As she started falling, a single thought entered her mind.

I chose poorly. Why didn't I listen to my AI?

Nevien Gospecker came in low over the Acid Plains. His communications halo chirped as he positioned the ship between the cauldron of bubbly acid and the arid deserts. Coming in low enough for the scrub hogs and tattle weasels to try to make a meal of his hunter's vessel was more than fun. It was titillating.

One more run out of the wastes and I'll have my debt to that fat cat paid.

A message appeared on his heads-up display. It read: *"Pick up num-nuts; I have a job for ya!"*

Moments later, the halo chime resumed. He decided to answer. It was Nymph. He felt a scowl forming on his face. *This one's relentless.*

An image of a female gnome appeared in his display. Her features were more of a human than a gnome, which made her stand out. Nevien surmised she was a half-breed. He wondered what it would be like to have a sexual relationship with a gnome. He never had, despite the fact that Nymph lived up to her nickname. She was like a restless spirit in the night.

"What can I help you with now?" Nevien asked.

"Hey, I thought you could use some work to pay off your

debt. I guess I was wrong. Shall I tell Nimsheer that you have the rest of your nut?"

Dammed workaholic gnomes. "Not yet, but I have a big job lined up. Enough to put us both on easy street."

"Oh, do you think we're hitched or something?"

"Your commission will be in the six-figure range."

"Until it's seven, I have to keep working for that slave driver," Nymph said.

"Well, I think we should discuss it over drinks tonight. I know this place—"

"No time. The boss is really pissed about this one."

"What's the job?"

"An inventor let his creation run amok in the city."

"Isn't that a job for the city patrol?"

"Nah, they only care about the plaza and other high-wealth areas. This thing is causing havoc in the industrial zone."

"How much does this job pay?"

"Double your usual."

"I hope you mean one hundred thousand."

The screen went blank. After a moment, Nymph reappeared with a smug look on her face.

"I got you sixty, and you'd better take it. It won't be on the table much longer."

"Alright, you win, but you owe me that drink."

"We'll talk after you bag this. It shouldn't be too hard for a big boy," Nymph said, grinning.

The screen went blank.

Someday, I will get to see what she's like in the sack.

Nevien opened the dossier. A picture of an inventor standing next to a robot over twice his height appeared. The gnome had an arrogant look about him.

If the council is paying top dollar for a bounty hunter like me, then this gnome is in deep shit.

A map with the approximate location replaced the photo of the gnome and his pet.

Nevien turned his ship toward the city, narrowly missing a burst from an acid-shooting geyser. He pulled the ship above the range of the acid shooters and turned on the autopilot so he could examine the mission files. Nymph had marked the map with several points of interest where the bot had already struck. Most of the attacks seemed to be isolated to the industrial complex below the city. There was no way he was going to navigate his ship in there. He would try to land in the East Landing Zone. In addition to cheap docking fees, hover speeders were available at an affordable price.

It's going to be tight.

An alarm sounded once he cleared the barrier wall. He switched to manual control as he flew over a reddish muck that would devour any living organism unlucky enough to fall in. He nicknamed it the "Bog of Death." Not too many made their approach to the city from the south because of that hazard, but he didn't have hours to wait on the northern border near the Seminal Forest.

"Oh shit!"

A red gas cloud was forming near the landing zone. Usually, the gas stayed in predictable patterns, but something was wrong. Fortunately, he maneuvered around the cloud and landed without incident.

That was a little too close.

▭

Beck followed Dr. Pekatin toward a private land cruiser. She marveled at the size of the gigantic campus as they sped toward the academy buildings. A platoon of cadets marched nearby. They seemed to be equally divided between men and women.

Moments later, the cruiser stopped at a private entrance. A few people her age were nearby; they appeared to be taking various tours as well. A fit green-skinned Trilliaxian caught her eye. The man appeared to be just a few years older and had a commanding appearance. A woman about his age was talking with him. Her features made it difficult to determine where she was from, but Beck's best guess was somewhere in the outer rim.

"Dr. Pekatin, I didn't know you were going to be visiting the academy," a large, stocky man with a wide midsection said.

Beck stared at the newcomer's admiral insignia in awe.

"I'm showing Rebecca, Duke Ampfere's daughter, around. This is her first visit to Sol-86."

"Excellent. It's great to meet you, Rebecca. I'm Nellus. What will you be studying?"

"I expect to be placed in the officer candidate school once my application is finalized."

"Excellent. We can always use good commanding officers." Nellus looked at his watch. "If you will excuse me, I'm speaking to the graduating class in half an hour. If you're not in a hurry, why don't you attend?"

"Yes, I would love that," Beck said.

The admiral motioned for them to follow. Her eyes darted about like a kid gazing upon sweets for the first time. Several naval officers that she recognized from her studies were in attendance. *I bet all these famous commanders are here for the graduation ceremonies.*

Most of the crowd gave the admiral's entourage room as they strode through the hallways leading to the graduation ceremony. Many cadets gave her looks of astonishment.

They are probably wondering who I am, but they will know soon enough—when I'm leading them into battle.

After a series of interior hallways, Nellus led them into an outdoor promenade. Plants and trees were planted at the edge of the hallways, giving the area a tropical look and feel.

"The actual ceremony will take place at the arena, about ten kilometers away. We can ride together in my private shuttle."

Moments later, Beck was gazing upon the academy from above. She knew the academy was big, but this place was enormous.

"After the ceremony, I'm hosting a party for a group of top students. It might be good to hear about their academy experiences," Nellus said.

"Well, I will need to get the Duke's permission, but I don't see a problem with that," Dr. Pekatin said.

"It would be an honor to be your guest," Beck added.

After the shuttle landed, Admiral Nellus was whisked away by a couple of advisors. Beck thought she heard something about an insurgent but couldn't be sure. The doctor led them to a seating area behind the podium. Beck's breath caught when she took in the size of the graduating class.

There must be at least a thousand students here.

The admiral delivered a riveting speech about self-awareness and preparedness. He even shared a few stories from when he was a green ensign ready to take on the universe and mentioned the civil war that had nearly destroyed Sol-86. Beck was impressed with his command of the audience. A thunderous applause echoed through the arena as the admiral concluded. If she'd had any doubt about becoming a commander, it was swept away by Nellus's speech.

"I've secured rooms for us at the guest quarters, not far from the student housing," Dr. Pekatin said.

"I still haven't had a chance to tour the launch pad and shuttle bay."

"In due time, my dear. We need to get some rest for our journey back to Quartus in the morning."

"I don't understand why we can't tour the facility now. We're here already, and I don't want to miss another opportunity."

Dr. Pekatin rubbed his chin as if in deep thought. Then he motioned for Beck to follow; and for the next three hours, Beck was treated to a tour of the facility. She got to see every division up close, and her only regret was that she wasn't already living there. She allowed herself to be escorted back to the shuttle. She watched the sunset on the western horizon as they rose away from the station. Soon she would be at the academy for real, and she hoped it would be sooner than later. Later that evening, Beck and Dr. Pekatin finished the tour of the academy. She'd wanted to see everything in detail. The doctor looked exhausted but didn't complain.

CHAPTER 6

BECK ENTERED THE JUDGING CHAMBER. No one was present. She hadn't thought anyone would be, since it was hours since the last council session. *Time for a late-night training session.*

For a moment, Beck's eyes were drawn to the Quartus's peaceful-looking surface. Then three robotic assassins with long arms and legs entered the chamber.

"En garde!"

Beck snapped out of her thoughts as the robot attackers moved in. A rapier materialized in her hands. She didn't know how the simulation functioned, but she always seemed to get the correct weapon for the fight at hand. One of the robots attempted to impale her with some kind of rod. She sliced the robot's hand off with her blade. She wouldn't have thought that cutting into metal with her weapon would have such a profound effect, but it was like she was cutting into human flesh. Another robot snuck up from behind and sliced its blade into her flesh. She activated her personal shield just as a third bot attacked from above.

Argh, that fucking hurt. These bots are learning.

She severed an arm from the lead attack bot, a leg from the second, and the head from the third. A severed mechanical arm seized her shin. She kicked it off, then threw the blade into the lead robot's head. The remaining appendages stopped moving.

If I didn't know any better, I'd say that some advanced artificial intelligence is at work here.

Beck's skin glistened with sweat. She longed to take a hot shower, then read her book on famous space battles. She was fascinated by the decisions past generals, admirals, and commanders had made to keep their soldiers safe. She promised herself she would protect anyone under her command, but that seemed like a million light-years away. She forced herself to continue her training; the old generals would have to wait.

"You're getting better, Becca," a strong voice said, breaking her train of thought.

She shot a glance in its direction. It was her father.

He never visits me, let alone watches my practice sessions.

"You honor me with your presence, Father," Beck said as she bowed.

Her father gave her a stern look of approval. She knew when he was displeased, and this look was different. She wondered if she would ever be good enough for him. But if this was the only praise she would get from the man, she would gladly take it.

"Thank you, Father."

"You received a communiqué from Sol-86 this afternoon."

"And you know the outcome?" Beck said.

"I do."

Her father gave her a regretful look. It was almost as if he was sorry for ever doubting her. She could be reading him wrong, but she doubted it. She knew he'd rather lose his arm than show his true feelings. His position demanded that he be unwavering, and as long as Beck could remember, he had been that and more.

"And did I get accepted?"

Her father nodded and gave the briefest of smiles. "Soon you will embark on a journey of epic proportions. It is not only the beginning of your next chapter but the end of this one. Before I say anything else, do you understand?"

"Yes, Father."

"Then let me be the first to congratulate you. I couldn't be prouder."

The muscles in Beck's throat constricted, and tears flowed from her eyes. She hated betraying the resolute mask she usually wore, but she hugged her father and wept. "Thank you, Father. It means more than you could ever know."

After a long moment, the duke broke away.

"You will leave in the morning. Be well, my daughter. I am so proud."

He left before she could say another word.

Cassidy's gnomish hair flapped like a condom wrapper in the wind.

Why would this fucking game spawn me in the air?

Cassidy's eyes watered. From her vantage point, the city stretched on for miles in every direction. Flying vehicles zoomed above and below her position. She was admiring a gigantic mountain that loomed above the city when a gusty breeze pushed her between two buildings. She nearly crashed into a glass skyscraper but spotted some scaffolding left over from some errant window washers farther down. A rope dangled in the wind. She pulled up her HUD and reviewed her skills. A timer counting down from eight made her feel anxious, but she suppressed the feeling. The rope was likely out of reach, but she decided to go for it. What was the worst that could happen? She activated the Sharp Mind skill with seconds remaining on the timer.

Everything slowed and seemed to bend. She wondered if she could will the rope to her. She knew that was silly, but these roguish skills were starting to grow on her. A red arrow showing the most direct path to the rope appeared. She was falling, but somehow she knew if she applied just the correct amount of energy into an action, her body would respond in different ways.

She used 5 percent of her remaining 49 percent of energy to take the first action and propelled herself sideways toward the scaffolding. The rope was still out of reach, so she applied another 10 percent of energy to ricochet off the scaffold. The motion from the counteraction caused the scaffolding to slam against the building. She stepped on the edge, and its momentum pushed her in the rope's direction. She caught it.

Holy crap, I can't believe that I did that. Parkour Online has nothing on us.

The motion caused the rope to swing into the traffic of the flying vehicles. She almost got splattered on the hood of more than a few shuttles. She thought she heard some lewd remarks as she swung on the rope. Movement caught her eye. A metal humanoid scaling a smooth spire nearby turned in her direction and laughed. It was at least ten feet tall.

"The admiral will pay for my master's impertinence."

What the hell is this crazy machine talking about?

A siren blared through the city. The metal man steadied itself on the top of the spire and pointed its arm. Moments later, its oversize hand propelled like a guided missile toward a glass building.

"Hang on to your ass, partner," the giant humanoid said in a booming voice.

The building exploded in a shower of glass and metal. Cassidy thought she saw people falling through the air.

"We have a mess on aisle seven. It's raining gnomes!"

That robot is crazy!

Cassidy had a lot of experience with machines in her life acting strangely, but nothing like this.

"What, this puny gnome?" the robot said as it launched more missiles at a stone building with a giant statue of a gnome. Despite the building being far away, the impact was deafening.

I need to find a way to stop that crazy bot.

<<>>

New Mission: Stop Megabot before It Destroys Senate Plaza

Primary Objective: Stop the insane bot before it destroys Senate Plaza.

Mission Details: The Megabot menace is threatening innocent lives. Expect to lose a significant amount of experience points if it harms Senate Plaza. Capturing, disabling, or killing it before then may grant additional experience and bonus loot.

Do you accept?

<<>>

"I accept the mission," Cassidy said.

Didn't I level up before? She checked her notifications and retrieved the following message:

<<>>

Congratulations! You have leveled up. You are now Level 2.
+18 Health
+10 Stamina

You have gained 10 attribute points. Please distribute them now.

<<>>

After some thought, Cassidy decided to allocate her points somewhat evenly. She put two points into Agility, two into Constitution, another two into Dexterity, two into Luck, and the final two into Strength.

<<>>

System Message: Please choose a new skill. The following skills are available:

Magician: An opportunity to hone your roguish skills. Use sleight-of-hand techniques to win any card game or to trick a mark. High Dexterity and Charisma attributes will yield additional bonuses.

Unhinged: Need to know if a trap exists before stepping into it? Use this skill to detect and disarm traps. As a bonus, additional loot may be found when using this skill.

Athlete: Ever wish you could be better at parkour or track and field? Both are combined when using this skill. Soon you will be scaling walls and jumping over rooftops. No spiderwebs required.

<<>>

Cassidy picked the Athlete skill without another thought. If she was going to catch a maniacal narcissistic robot that scaled buildings, then she would need to rely on as many physical skills as she could get her hands on.

And how in the hell am I going to do that?

She felt hopeless. She had no confidence that she would be able to stop Megabot in time. But Joe was also in this instance somewhere, and she would never live it down if he won.

Cassidy inspected the contents of her inventory. She had made the mistake of not checking before and found two items there that would have been useful: a grappling hook and a pair of red boots with white lightning bolts stitched into the sides.

"How did I get these?" Cassidy said.

A cat meowed and a dog barked, which were the only responses she got. In the distance, she heard crashes, screams from unsuspecting victims, and the maniacal laughter of an insane robot. She sighed as she swung over to a nearby ledge. She scanned the boots with her interface.

<<>>

System Message: Since you're an athlete, we have chosen something to get you across the finish line. Behold the Flotsam Fliers:

Agility +5
Athlete +5
Health Regeneration +5%
Stamina Regeneration +10%

This is an exceptionally rare item.

From your friends at Interstellar Online.

<<>>

Cassidy put on the boots and felt an overwhelming urge to run. Her eyes wandered to the grappling hook device. Then it all came together. She took a hesitant step toward the Megabot menace and traveled the space of a hundred feet in a matter of moments. It was like walking but at a pace that most automobiles would travel. She cringed at the thought of losing control at that speed but still ran toward the disturbance in the distance. When she came to the end of a building, she jumped and held her breath as she leaped dozens of feet across the empty expanse.

CHAPTER 7

Rebecca stared at the brownish planet below her. It had taken her years of preparation and a great deal of heartache, but she was finally heading to the academy as a pupil.

"I hope you are ready for the challenges to come, my dear," a familiar voice said.

Beck turned to see Dr. Pekatin, the royal physician. "Hello, what brings you here, Doctor?"

"I came at your father's behest. The training here can get a little rough."

"I can handle myself," Beck said.

"I don't doubt your abilities, Your Highness, but protocols—"

"Damn your protocols. When we are on Sol-86, you shall obey my orders," Beck interrupted.

"I understand."

"We are initiating the landing sequence in two minutes. Please return to your seats and strap in for landing," the pilot said over the intercom.

Various military personnel assigned to guard the royal escort returned to their seats. The doctor made his way to the cabin reserved for diplomats and traveling royalty. He stopped short of entering the private chamber.

"Are you coming ... Your Highness?"

"You can ride in the lap of luxury. I prefer to stay with my men," Beck said as she took a position between two grunts.

The enormous man to her left gave Beck a hard look. "I think you are in the wrong section ... ma'am."

"I'm where I need to be. With my men," Beck said.

"Suit yourself, but don't come crying if you break a nail."

Beck ignored the implied insult. The ship dropped hundreds of feet without warning.

"Woo-hoo! I love how this drop makes my balls feel," one soldier said.

The ship rocked as it tore through the atmosphere. Beck flipped the blast shield attached to her helmet into the down position. She wouldn't be able to see with her eyes, but she could see through the heads-up display interface. She opted for the outside view of her shuttle as they descended. She didn't want to miss any of the action. Someday she would pilot her own ship and lead men into battle, and she wanted—needed—to know what it felt like.

"Whoa, this is rougher than normal," another soldier said.

"Do you want me to hold you, baby?" a burly soldier replied.

"Fuck you, Melson," the smaller soldier said.

"Quit whining, you pussy. We have a female here, and she's not bitching."

The ship was covered in flames. Military ships had a special coating that protected them against damage during landings, and Beck reasoned that some kind of friction had caused the flames. She made a mental note to find out what the process was.

Every captain of a ship needs to know her vessel inside and out.

Two black ships that looked to her like falcons positioned themselves in the same free-fall pattern as her ship, the *Reconnoiterer.*

This is not standard military protocol. What the hell are these guys up to?

Moments later, the ship fired upon her vessel. The hull cracked, and the front portion separated. Before she could react, the ship was torn in half as easily as if it were so much paper. The pilot and the doctor and anyone else in the front part of the craft were gone.

"We're under attack. It's the outworlders," Melson said.

Beck flipped up her blast shield. What was left of the ship had sped up to an unsafe velocity.

"Who are these outworlders?"

"Trouble; screw this. I'm bolting," the skinny soldier said.

The man pulled something from his chair. A deafening blast was followed by the man getting ejected away from the ship. Most of the soldiers followed suit. The falcon ships reappeared. They opened fire on the descending soldiers.

"Those men are helpless. They didn't have a chance," Beck said.

"They jumped too soon," Melson said.

Beck's access to the ship's controls had been severed when the ship got ripped apart, and she could see the planet's surface approaching fast. Beck closed her eyes and started the familiar mantra that she was so accustomed to. If she was going to die, she wanted to do so without any burdens. Her spirit would be unencumbered in the afterlife, whatever that was. Then, as suddenly as the ship had begun to fall, it stopped. The straps dug into her chest, pulling her back into her seat. She couldn't breathe. Moments later, the pain eased. The vessel rocked as an unseen force pulled it.

"We are caught in a tractor beam."

"They won't take me alive," Beck said as she removed her sidearm from its holster.

"Don't give these sadistic fucks any reason," Melson said.

"So are we just going to surrender?"

"I see no other choice."

"I don't accept that. As long as we draw breath, there is another way."

"I love your gusto, kid, and you are braver than my men, but you need to be smarter than that."

"What does that mean?"

"The outworlders are sadistic and cruel. They will kill you in the worst way imaginable if you resist."

The ship landed hard atop a mountain. Two men appeared in black leather outfits. Seconds later, both men were upon her. One man slapped her, then confiscated her weapon. Beck thought she noticed a look of sheer pleasure. The other man shot Melson in the face. She could only stare at the bloody aftermath, then burned the men's faces into her memory. One man looked to be in his forties and had black hair and a scar that ran across his left cheek. The other man looked much younger, in his twenties, and had blond hair with no distinguishing features. Both men laughed.

"Look what you've done. You're going to pay for that—Your Highness."

"What I've done?" Beck said, incredulous.

She lunged toward the men and punched the older man. The uppercut caused the man to fall on his ass. The other man grabbed one of her hands, and she responded by backhanding him. An intense shocking sensation coursed through her body.

The older man had jabbed a short electrified bar into her side. She tried to raise a fist but couldn't move; it felt like every muscle in her body was under attack.

One of the men shoved a black bag over her head. Moments later, something hit her hard, and darkness enveloped her.

CHAPTER 8

The view from the industrial district was interesting. A combination of old and new structures surrounded her. With her in-game interface, she pulled up a map of Seminal City. Megabot had had a considerable head start and was doing its best to cause as much havoc as possible. Although Cassidy had no evidence that the mad bot had injured or even killed anyone, she wasn't prepared to take that chance. She pushed harder, her speed increased, and the surrounding scenery blurred. Just as she thought about slowing, a massive dirigible came into view. It looked like a giant balloon with ropes strung across it. She tried slowing, but she had too much momentum to stop. She smacked into the side of the vessel. Black spots that looked like floating holes swirled around her head as she began to slide, then got caught up in a tangle of rope.

Is this what it's like to see stars?

"Hey, gorgeous," a familiar, squeaky voice said.

Much to her dismay, the owner of the voice was the annoying inventor that had birthed the menace into the world. The gnome reached down and held out a hand. She stretched, but it was too far to reach.

"Come on, baby. Stretch," Ufao said.

"I'm stuck. It's as far as I can go."

The male gnome got up and unzipped his pants.

"What the hell are you doing?"

"Providing some motivation? Most women find my succulent cock irresistible," Ufao said. The gnome smiled as he pulled down his britches and smallclothes. Cassidy couldn't believe what she was seeing. Ufao's schlong was enormous. He smiled as his member came to attention.

That thing's longer than my forearm!

"Put that away and help me up."

"Yes, that's the idea. I want to mount my vessel," Ufao said, chuckling.

In your dreams.

A moment later, the gnome fished in his pants and pulled out a small metal box. His tongue darted in and out like a snake as he fiddled with it. A drone flew toward her, then started cutting the rope with a laser. Her body broke free, and her hand slipped. She fell several feet. The drone dived and slipped beneath her.

"Em, I do envy that drone sometimes," Ufao said, smiling.

She hung on for dear life as the gnome navigated the drone and her onto the dirigible's deck. Ufao shuffled toward Cassidy with his pants bunched up at his ankles, his boner swaying in the wind.

"Raging pumpersnuffs. What are you doing out here?" Ufao asked.

"Not much, just trying to stop the menace your ego created. Now put that thing away before you hurt yourself."

"Is that a bit of sarcasm I sense?" Ufao said. "With women, I can never tell."

Cassidy rolled her eyes. "You're not going to win over anyone with that attitude. But we have more pressing matters than trying to get you laid."

The gnome turned a shade of crimson as he pulled his pants up.

"Come on. Even with this oversize balloon, we can catch up to Megabot in no time," Cassidy said.

"I think you misunderstand. I'm not going after Renfrey. He's gone mad. I'm skipping town before I get arrested."

"Don't you want to at least help clean up your mess?" Cassidy said.

"Well, maybe if you give me a little something in return?"

"Like what?"

The gnome grinned sheepishly. "You know, a little rub and tug?"

Unbelievable. We are pursuing his creation, and he wants a hand job?

"Maybe later, but you have to help before the situation gets out of hand."

"No, I want it in your hand," Ufao said.

Cassidy gave the gnome a tired look. "Just turn this thing around before I throw you off of it."

The gnome's eyes widened as a horn blared in the distance. Cassidy followed his gaze. A tall glass structure collapsed as they argued. She struck the gnome on the back of the head. "I'm not going to tell you again. Move toward Renfrey—now!"

"Okay, boss lady. And for the record, I like being hit by a feisty woman. But Renfrey will not have a chance once I detonate this," Ufao said, waving a device that resembled a stopwatch.

"What's that?"

"Oh, just a little insurance policy that will stop that mad robot in his tracks. One press of this button and Megabot self-destructs—we just need to get close enough first."

"I'm probably going to regret asking, but how close?"

"Line of sight; within fifty yards should be enough. But the closer the better, because there's just enough juice for one detonation attempt. Then it's back to manual control, I'm afraid," Ufao said sheepishly.

"Then we better get a move on."

"Yes, ma'am. I aim for you to please me."

Ufao turned the craft in the direction of Megabot. Cassidy estimated that they would reach the damned robot in under ten minutes and started searching the cargo hold for anything useful. Other than sealed barrels and empty crates, she didn't find anything. As she scaled the ladder to the upper decks, something wet fell on her. It felt like a sticky and wet balloon. To her dismay, a used sex toy with blond hair and a gaping hole for a mouth was staring at her.

What the fuck? It figures that this horny gnome would have a sex toy floating around.

The thought gave her an idea. She scaled the ladder and found Ufao steering the flying boat in the direction of a massive flame.

"What happened?" Cassidy asked, pointing at the flame.

"My bot is cocking everything up today. It's almost at Senate Plaza. If he destroys that, I might as well move to the ass end of the Smuggler's Moon."

"Hold on. We are going turbo," Ufao said.

The gnome flipped some switches and pressed some buttons. Cassidy heard a creaking noise. The ship shook; then she was knocked off her feet as the engines kicked into high gear.

"Argh!"

She hit the side of the ship so hard the wind got knocked out of her. Ufao held on to the steering mechanism for dear life. Cassidy snatched a glance at the plaza. It was approaching so rapidly that if they didn't do something, they would overshoot Megabot.

"Slow down!" Cassidy said.

The gnome looked like he was having a difficult time reaching the controls. They were moments away from the plaza, and the ship wasn't slowing. An explosion suddenly rocked the vessel, which slowed and veered away from the plaza. Cassidy noticed smoke from the aft side of the ship. Next to the control panel was a huge button with a red stripe running through the middle.

Is that an emergency stop button?

She had just enough energy to activate her Athlete skill. She spanned the thirty feet in a second and smashed the button. The ship stopped, shook some more, then exploded. The last thing she remembered was the gnome grasping her leg as they fell to their deaths.

CHAPTER 9

THE BLACK BAG SMELLED FOUL, like someone had gotten sick in it and then left it in the sun too long. Beck wanted to vomit but tried to hold it together.

These men just want to frighten you. Don't give in.

"I can't believe we caught the princess so easily. You told me this game was difficult," one man said.

"She didn't even put up a fight. I expected a shoot-out at the very least. Are we going to turn her in for the bounty?"

What are they talking about? There's a bounty on my head?

"Not yet ... Maybe we can have a little fun with her first."

"While she's tied up?"

"Nah! That's no fun. I want her to beg for it."

"She looks like a military badass to me. I'm sure she can kick both our asses."

"She's just a girl. I'd like to see her try."

Another round of laughter from the men. Rough hands pulled her arms. A moment later, she was on her feet. She stumbled as she tripped on some debris. Light shone from the bottom of the sack. She moved her head slightly until her feet were visible. She appeared to be walking on gravel. Beck shivered as an icy breeze bit into her flight suit. They walked for a long time before the gravel turned into shiny metal. Even with the black bag over her head, Beck had to squint to avoid the reflection of the metal in the sunlight.

"Who is this?" a female voice asked.

"Nelson's hunch paid off. The shuttle contained royalty."

"Take it off."

Moments later, Beck's vision was assaulted by the sudden admittance of light. To Beck, it seemed like it took an eternity to see anything. Directly in front of her was a tall woman dressed in a brown robe. Her golden complexion emanated a warm radiance that Beck couldn't place.

"Who are you?" Beck asked.

"My name is Jannumar," the woman said as she removed her robe.

The woman had the most fit body Beck had ever seen. She wore golden bikini panties and a bra that showed as much cleavage as possible.

How is she not cold? I'm freezing, and I'm fully clothed.

The older captor reached out and touched the bronze-skinned beauty's ass. She slapped him. "Stay in character, Ronny. Don't spoil this for me. You shall have your fun later."

"Man, I need to get laid. Donald said the AI constructs give out poontang like candy," the younger guard said.

Jannumar shot the younger guard a murderous look. The older guard punched the other guard in the gut.

"Ow! Why did you do that?"

"The lady said to stay in character, and that's what you are going to do if you don't want to get vaporized."

"Fuck, Ron, that hurt. I'm going to have bruises once I take off the gear."

"Remember, she's not a PC," Ron said.

"What's a PC?" Beck asked.

"A player character—"

Ron hit the younger man so hard he went flying several feet into the air. He landed on his back and moaned as he moved slightly.

"Is he alright?" Beck asked.

"Yeah, he will live. Won't you, Jonny?" Ron said as he kicked the fallen soldier.

"This is unbecoming behavior for a man in the uniform you wear. I doubt you are truly part of the royal guard," Beck said.

"You got that right, Princess."

"You shall address me properly as 'Princess Rebecca' or simply 'Your Royal Highness,'" Beck said.

Ron smiled, revealing some missing teeth.

"Remove her bindings. She's not a prisoner. Bring her to the throne room," Jannumar said.

Beck watched the woman turn and enter a building that resembled a spire. It stretched upward as far as she could see. In the distance behind it was an enormous mountain with snowy peaks.

"Give me your hands," Ron said.

The soldier unlocked her bindings, and she felt an immediate need to rub her wrists. She hugged herself and rubbed at her extremities as a brisk breeze swept through the terrace.

Why aren't these people affected by the cold? And what is a player character?

These were questions that Beck filed away. These strange people were not from any sector in the galaxy that she knew. If they were from Alpha Proxima, that could explain the strange clothes and mannerisms, but they seemed even more eccentric than that.

"Move."

Beck was pushed in the direction of the building. Movement to her left caught her eye. It was a spaceport next to a gigantic city. Ships were landing at regular intervals. She reasoned that she must be close to Sol-86's capital city. Ron and Jonny accompanied Beck into the massive structure.

"What is this place?" Beck asked.

"It's known as Keng Citadel. It's one of the many strongholds the galactic military still has left," Ron said.

"Which military is that? You don't belong to any house I know."

Ron seemed unsure of himself. "Well, you should speak with Jannumar about that. She knows the game—I mean the system—better than I do."

"I understand the game," Beck said.

"What? You do?" Ron said in a confused tone.

"The politics of the throne have weighed heavily on us all," Beck said.

"Oh, yes. It has indeed," Ron said.

Beck gazed upon the interior of Keng Citadel with great interest. It was dark inside, but she could see statues of men she didn't know.

Every military compound in the Nupertian System has statues of the great generals. Yet I don't know who these guys are.

They loomed menacingly overhead like jackals waiting to pounce. She had never heard of this place, and she had studied Sol-86 in detail. But she still had a lot to learn. In the distance, basking in the soft radiance that could only be the sun's glory, was Jannumar. She sat on a massive throne that was considerably larger than Beck's father's. At first glance, she looked naked, but she wasn't. The string bikini matched her skin and didn't hide much of her more private areas. The woman was fascinating.

Despite that, a feeling of overwhelming dread overcame Beck as she approached what she thought of as the golden throne. She was determined to find out who these people really were. If Jannumar wanted a conversation, she would give her one.

It'll probably be more like an interrogation.

The men stopped about ten feet from the throne. An absent wave from Jannumar sent the men on their way.

"Oh, where are my manners? Would you like to sit?" Jannumar asked.

"If it's all the same to you, I'd rather stand," Beck said.

"Very well. Let's start by getting to know each other. I know your name is Beck and you are royalty, but that's it. Care to expand?"

I'm not telling the enemy anything. "Cadet Rebecca Ampfere, assigned to the Sol-86 Academy for infantry training."

Jannumar frowned. "That's not what I meant. Where are you from?"

"I'm Rebecca Ampfere—"

"Yes, we've established that already. I will tell you my truth. I'm from a tribe only known as the Protectors of the Light, which is a group of religious zealots run by Sunarmar, my brother. We are descendants of an ancient race known as the Mazzalothians."

Beck had heard stories about that ancient race. It was rumored they were the oldest species in the galaxy, perhaps the universe.

Jannumar gave her a curious look. "What planet are you from?"

I shouldn't tell her anything, but I need to know where she is from, and it's no secret where House Ampfere is from. "My house hails from Quartus."

The bronze-skinned woman made some strange hand signals. "Ah, the blue planet with the three moons."

What was she doing with her hands? It seemed like she was looking something up in a holo-book.

"What were you doing with your hands?" Beck asked.

Jannumar's eyes widened. "You saw that?"

Beck nodded.

"I'm testing a new retinal lens that allows me to retrieve information without a tablet."

Hmm, I will need to look into that.

A siren blared from the city.

"What's happening?" Beck asked.

"I ... don't know." Jannumar swiped frantically in the air. The woman looked like she was trying to put a puzzle together in midair. "The city is under attack?"

A red portal opened in front of Beck. Three guards burst through. Beck recognized two of them.

"What's that thing you just came through?"

Before anyone could respond, a one-eyed behemoth poked a massive arm through the portal and grabbed the guard she didn't know. With one chomp, the man was decapitated. The giant drank the man's blood. The portal closed, sawing the guard in half. Beck took a few steps back.

These people are magicians?

"Holy shit, what the hell just happened?" Jonny asked.

"It looks like someone hacked the game again. I bet it's the Fanaticals," Ron said.

"I agree something is off. Anyone know what's going on with this instance?"

"Yeah, someone set it to nightmare mode," Jannumar said.

Three more portals opened. Creatures of every kind imaginable poured out. Many looked like fantastical monsters from the stories her father told her. A fourth portal opened, and a man with gray skin and blue hair emerged. His eyes shifted to Beck, and he started running toward her. The man took something from his belt and threw it in Beck's direction. Moments later, she was trapped in some kind of sticky netting. It reminded her of the webs that certain bugs from Quartus, known as spimites, secreted.

"No! Die, traitor," Jannumar said to the gray-skinned man.

The bronze woman leaped in front of Beck. She swung two daggers toward the man. He removed a blaster and shot at Jannumar. To Beck's amazement, the woman deflected the blast with the blade, which glowed a nasty red. She yelped as the heat of the blade came into contact with her skin; then she dropped the weapon to the ground. Beck thought she could hear a hissing sound as it struck the floor. Jannumar threw her other blade at the intruder. He cried out as it struck his arm. Blue blood poured from his wound.

"Protect the princess!"

Ron fought the creatures while Jonny broke off to engage the intruder. The gray-skinned man released a glowing whip and, with the flick of his wrist, took Jonny's left arm off like a butcher carving a beast. Jonny screamed in pain. Ron broke off to assist, but it was too late. The intruder jumped on Beck; then, moments later, she was being pulled back. The chamber inside the citadel changed to a field with millions of stars. She could still see inside the citadel, but it was like peering into a window from a great distance. Beck's lungs ached as the air rushed out of them.

What's happening? I'm in space—without proper gear!

Icy fingers covered her body, and Beck wondered if this was what it was like to die.

What a waste.

Dead before she'd had a chance to prove herself. She had imagined herself dying in a blaze of glory while leading a squadron into battle, not being frozen in space! Her face felt like glass, being frozen faster than she had thought possible.

Soon it will be over.

Beck's body seized up. She could no longer feel anything. She closed her eyes and waited for the inevitable.

CHAPTER 10

Ufao danced naked in a meadow that stretched on for infinity. The beautiful gnome he had seen in the judging chamber sat there in all her glory. She had bigger breasts than most gnomes, but Ufao didn't mind. He wanted only the best for his future bride. Her long hair covered her breasts, but he was able to see her lower regions, and that made him tense—but in a good way. Ufao ran toward her. She gazed upon his massive cock. Smart gnomes had massive members, and he wanted to get his waxed to make it look even bigger. He was nearly to her when a clamorous booming sound emitted from everywhere. Clouds invaded the clear day and threatened a downpour.

"You shall not have her," a familiar voice boomed.

Before he could contemplate who the voice might have belonged to, Renfrey, his creation, snatched up his gnomish beauty and ran like the wind. Ufao tried to catch up, but a flow of black goo appeared from nowhere and knocked him off-balance. He tried to stop his fall, but his momentum already had him. He fell headlong into the muck.

Ufao awoke to pain. The last thing that he remembered was getting zapped by Renfrey.

Why did he betray me?

Before he could put another ounce of energy into that line of thought, the floor fell out from under him. He was standing in midair. The entire city was below him. It was like he was walking on another plane of existence.

I'm falling!

Ufao opened his eyes to find that his hand was halfway up the leg of the sexy gnome. It would have been a perfect moment if he had not been falling to his death. The gnome woman was reaching for something on her belt.

I don't think I could have sex in midair, but I'm willing to try. Now, I need to get in just the right position.

The female gnome shot at one of the walls. He couldn't tell what she was holding, but soon they were heading headlong into the wall she'd shot.

"What are you doing?" Ufao asked.

"Saving your scrawny ass. Now follow my lead."

The female gnome landed on the wall gracefully. Ufao tried his best to land on his feet but ended up smashing his side into the wall. It felt like someone was hitting him on the head, chest, and torso all at once. After several moments, the pain subsided enough for him to get his bearings. The female gnome was saying something, but he was so focused on his sudden onset of pain he wasn't paying attention to her.

"Are you coming or not? Your creation has entered the plaza!"

The kill switch. I almost forgot I had it. We need to get in range. Then I can activate his self-destruct.

"We need to get closer," Ufao said.

A horrific scraping noise came from Megabot's position. It appeared to be hugging an enormous statue.

"What in the hell is that thing doing?"

Ufao followed the female gnome's gaze. Megabot appeared to be humping the statue of one of Seminal City's founders.

I didn't program that into his logic circuits.

Ufao watched in horror as the statue crumbled. Somehow, Megabot was getting larger, and Ufao couldn't explain it. The metal alloy that he had used for Megabot could bend plus or minus 10 percent, but this growth was much larger. He hoped the self-destruct would still work.

"Grab onto my waist."

Ufao wrapped his arms around the female gnome. She was soft in all the right places, and his body responded to the intimacy. The female gnome shot her weapon at various buildings and billboards. She even latched on to a flying vehicle. They traveled a mile before the cable unlatched itself and they landed at the edge of Senate Plaza. Megabot was now at least thirty feet tall. Ufao did some quick mental math. The alloy that he had used was made out of trinetihum and aluminum. The result was a strong inner core with a flexible outer shell. Megabot was using the weaker metal to extend its reach. In reality, it wasn't growing but stretching.

"Time to turn off this thing," Cassidy said.

Ufao nodded, then reached for the remote control. He opened the safety lid, then pressed the red button. Other than an audible clicking sound, nothing happened.

"That should have worked!"

The female gnome rolled her eyes. "Why am I not surprised? You can't even program a simple kill switch. You're useless."

The female gnome ran toward the Megabot menace.

She's going to get killed!

"And what are you going to do about it?" a gnome that sounded like himself said.

"Who said that?"

"You don't know yourself very well, do you?"

Ufao shot a glance in the direction of the voice, and another gnome that looked just like him crossed his arms and looked angry.

I must have gotten hit harder than I thought. What an awful day this is!

"Yes, it is a terrible day. Now get off your ass and save her. You won't get laid sitting on the sidelines."

He reasoned that his subconscious was trying to communicate with him, and while this normally would have concerned him, he went with the notion that something else was at play. Before he could ponder its meaning, a group of marauders entered the plaza. Some had golden skin and wore revealing clothing that showed much of their bodies. The golden-skinned ones were leading a group of uniformed men into the center of the plaza. He thought he recognized them, but he couldn't place where they might have come from. The Acid Plains? He couldn't remember. Explosions detonated all around the plaza. Bodies resembling the city guard were thrown in all directions.

Beck found herself in a white room with no windows or doors. The only furnishing was a white throne occupied by a rather unattractive man with few clothes.

"Hello, Rebecca!"

Beck backed up several steps and nearly fell.

"Relax, you've been freed from the clutches of a space witch."

"What are you talking about?

The man laughed. "You're Miss Delgado's AI, but I call you my bargaining chip."

"How did I get here? And who are you?"

"I summoned you. I don't expect you to understand all the technical details, but consider this your draft card."

"I don't understand."

"You will. Just let me explain."

She stared into the skinny man's eyes. Her father had taught her to confront an enemy head-on, and that by looking into their eyes, a door to their soul would be revealed. In truth, Beck just wanted to avoid looking at the man's junk. The skinny man's lack of clothing made that all but impossible unless she was staring into his eyes.

"What do you say to that?"

"I—don't know," Beck said.

The man laughed. "You don't get it, but never mind about that. I have a proposition for you."

"Such as?"

"Your Mazzalothian friends are fighting to the death as we speak. I know you want an opportunity to prove yourself."

"How would you know that?"

"Ah, but I'm the game master. I know all."

"Who are you?"

"I am called many things, but you may call me Zart ... Tender."

I know that name, but from where?

"I know your face, but I can't place it."

"Not a big follower of the royal family, I take it?"

"What are you talking about?" Beck asked.

"My father is Eldrich—"

"The emperor?"

Zart smiled.

"What do you want from me?" Beck asked.

"Like I said, I have a proposition for you. I need you to find someone for me."

"If you're related to the emperor, then can't you find them yourself?"

"I ... actually know where this person is. I just need you to get close to her. Once you do that, your victory will be assured."

"Victory over whom?"

"Why, the menace that has been terrorizing Seminal City!"

Beck gave him a blank stare.

"The metal man that your friends are fighting," Zart said.

Beck remembered Jannumar and her people discussing some threat. She wondered if they were fighting and how they were faring during the battle. "How do I find this person? I don't even know where to look."

Zart waved, and a picture of an attractive human female appeared. Her long auburn hair and blue eyes were captivating.

"Who is she? And why is she so important?"

"She's the fish that got away, but that's not important right now. Just give her this, and I will take care of the rest. Soon you will have the power to defeat the metal man."

Zart gave Beck a tiara that looked too small for an adult to wear. The moment she touched it, her vision clouded; then she was at the base of an enormous statue in the middle of a plaza. A gigantic metal man began hitting the bronze statue. A gonging sound emitted with each strike. Two gnomes shot some sort of grappling hook and tied up the metal man. The bindings lasted for a second before snapping. Lasers shot from its eyes, and the gnomes dodged the blasts with ease. However, the surrounding area wasn't as lucky. Gardens of pristine flowers caught fire and burned. Nearby buildings also combusted into flame.

Beck formulated a plan of attack. She would attack the metal man while he was distracted with the gnomes. Beck touched the signet ring of House Ampfere, and a protective armor enveloped her. She removed something from her belt that resembled a pair of brass knuckles. When she put them on, a glowing blue sword grew out of her hand.

Prepare to die, you metal menace.

Beck ran toward the metal man with her glowing sword in hand. The acrid odor of burning metal assaulted her nostrils. She screamed, raised her sword, and prepared to meet her destiny.

CHAPTER 11

Duke Ampfere strode into the council chamber, which was made up of glass and smooth curved metal columns. Below the duke's feet was the blue ball of a planet known as Quartus, his home world. He conducted most of the planet's affairs from the orbital space station above the planet. Since assuming the title of duke, the planet's resources had dwindled significantly. The oceans had been rising for generations, and the planet's surface was now more than 80 percent water. Environmentalist groups had threatened the duke's life for years, which was another reason for the duke's residence on the space station.

"All rise. The duke is now in attendance," a skinny man said.

The duke took his seat at the center of the chamber. "Thank you, Plannar. Can you please get the emperor so we can start?"

The skinny man tapped his tablet, then summoned a gigantic holographic image of a skinny man dressed in an elegant silk robe.

"Duke Ampfere, the council is not scheduled to meet until next month. Why have you called this emergency session?" Emperor Tender said.

"My daughter, Princess Ampfere, has gone missing, and new intelligence suggests that she has been captured by an enemy of the Nupertian System."

"Which enemy? Do you know?"

"According to spies on Sol-86, she was captured by the Protectors of the Light."

"Never heard of them. What makes you think they are enemies of the system and not just your house?"

"The Protectors of the Light are descendants of the Mazzalothians."

"Who?"

"You may know them as the Ancients."

"Oh, those guys," Emperor Tender said as he rubbed his chin.

"Either way, capturing a member of any royal house is a treasonous offense, is it not?"

"Yes—punishable by death. You may have a company of elite Zerkar troops. I will have the captain in charge report to you as soon as they are ready."

"Thank you, Your Imperial Majesty."

The emperor waved his hand in a dismissive gesture.

"If you can, I want the leader of these Protectors of the Light brought to me in Zartander," the emperor said.

"It shall be done," the duke said.

Moments later, the hologram of the emperor disappeared.

"Prepare a room for the war effort."

"I thought this was a rescue operation," Plannar said.

"Anyone that captures my baby girl has asked for war on not only themselves but their entire species. Have the joint generals brought to the war room."

The duke hurried out of the chamber. The people of Quartus were already at the breaking point, and a war with such a just cause would solidify his reign for years to come.

Baldor slid onto the platform that would take him to his ship. The duke of Quartus had asked for help from someone in charge of Sol-86, and since the planet Trillix was the highest authority in that system, the responsibility fell to him. Baldor sneered at the thought of involving himself in the affairs of the duke. This should be a family matter, but it would gain Baldor significant political capital if he lent some support.

Or I could send a proxy in my stead.

He called the royal assistant.

"Yes, Your Highness? How can I help today?" a green humanoid figure said.

"I need a proxy, someone with military experience, to travel to Quartus to represent the Trilliaxians."

"Commander Dreg is exploring the dead space region, but Stev is available."

"What about my firstborn?" Baldor said.

"Devron is studying engineering at the Sol-86 Academy and is not reachable."

"Dammit, this is a job for a firstborn Trilliaxian. But Stev will do. Thank you, daughter."

He would let his son handle this. And besides, he had better things to do. Like officiating the grand opening of the first intergalactic coitus ceremony.

CHAPTER 12

Cassidy and Ufao landed a hundred or so feet from the raging Megabot. People ran in every direction to avoid getting squashed by flying debris or anything else that the robot was flinging.

"Can you try using your deactivation device again?" Cassidy said.

Ufao gave her a blank stare. It was like he was shell-shocked. She kicked the gnome in the shin.

"Argh, what did you do that for?"

"I needed to wake you up. Now, deactivate this fucker before he gets too far into the city."

He rummaged into his pocket and brought out the remote. It was cracked in many places. Cassidy's heart sank as she watched the gnome take the device apart.

"Just a moment. I think I have it now—no!"

"What's the matter?"

"It's still not working. The frequency must have changed."

"I know about your little fail-safe, puny gnome. I recalibrated my logic circuits during my transformation. You are done," Megabot said, laughing.

Terrific!

Cassidy ran toward the metal man. Ufao called for her, but she ignored him. She had to find a way to trip him or something.

<<>>

System Message: Megabot is near Senate Plaza. Mission failure imminent.

<<>>

Two tall buildings were now between Megabot and Senate Plaza. It tried squeezing between them but got stuck. Cassidy shot her grappling hook toward one of the buildings, attempting to trip the giant robot. It snapped like a rubber band. Cassidy shot two more grappling hooks, pinning the metal menace to the wall of a building. It broke free.

"Ha! Your little net won't trap me, tiny gnome."

He's gotten bigger! How?

She reasoned that it was feeding off the destruction somehow. The more it destroyed, the more powerful it became. Its red eyes stared at her; then its brow seemed to furrow before the lasers came. She dodged, trying not to become a pile of ash. Cassidy could feel the rage coming off the metal man, and pain shot through her arm as a laser nicked her. Twenty percent of her health bar disappeared in an instant.

"We have to get out of here," Ufao said.

The two gnomes danced to avoid the deadly laser show. Then, as suddenly as it had begun, the lasers stopped, and Megabot screamed. Cassidy saw a blue glow out of the corner of her eye. Someone was hacking at Megabot's legs with some kind of glowing sword. Moments later, Cassidy found herself falling toward the shadowy figure with the sword.

"I will catch you!" a familiar voice said.

Ufao had inflated something that resembled a beanbag chair and was running toward her landing position. The figure with the sword leaped dozens of feet into the air and chopped Megabot's right arm off at the bend of the elbow. It roared.

"A little to the left," Cassidy said.

The gnome moved the makeshift chair into position, and Cassidy landed on it, then bounced to the hard and cold ground. Another 30 percent of health and 10 percent of her stamina disappeared. Some kind of oil rained down from the sky. A massive leg belonging to Megabot almost squashed her as the robot fought the figure with the sword.

That was too close!

Cassidy watched in awe as the person in the armor continued hacking Megabot to pieces. The bot got smaller as the fight continued, and it wasn't just because of the hacking and slashing of the shadowy presence.

"No, you do not know what you're doing! The admiral must die!" Megabot roared.

The shadowy figure stopped for a moment. The metal man positioned itself on one knee and raised its arms in a pleading gesture as it spoke quietly to the blade wielder.

"I got the deactivator working again!" Ufao said excitedly.

"Well, what are you waiting for? Use it!"

Ufao looked conflicted. "I can either deactivate Megabot, or I can rig the device to transmit what they are saying. It may provide some useful information for us. Your choice."

Cassidy considered for a moment. While she was interested in finding out what had made this shadowy figure and Megabot talk, she was determined to win the game. It had been far too long since she'd had a win. The last few play sessions had resulted in pleasing Joe more than herself. She was determined to change that.

"Nah, fuck it. Fry its metal ass."

Ufao pressed the Self-Destruct button. A flashing numeric display came to life and floated in the air above the device. Cassidy braced for something big as they waited for the countdown to hit zero.

"Explain yourself," Beck said.

"During my activation process, I downloaded all of Seminal City's knowledge and found evidence of a plot to eliminate a member of a high-ranking house. The evidence suggests that the admiral was acting at the behest of the emperor when he ordered it," Megabot explained.

"Who is the target?"

"Duke Ampere."

"Father?"

She pressed her sword into Megabot's chest. It was not enough to injure it but enough to drive the point home. "How do you know this? Tell me everything!"

"Your father is being manipulated into starting a war."

"War? With whom?"

A light shone out of the metal man's left eye. An image of a scantily clad woman appeared. Some male figures also came into view, but they were dressed in robes.

The woman in the image resembles Jannumar.

"What does that have to do with my father?"

"They plan to lure him out by capturing someone close to him. This will force the duke into action. The emperor and Admiral Nellus plan to use the moment as a distraction. Then they will—"

Megabot exploded in a series of sparks and flames. The

gnomes she had seen before jumped on the metal man and began zapping Megabot with some kind of device.

"I demand you to stop!" Beck said.

"Are you talking to us?" the female gnome replied.

"Yes, why did you attack the metal man? I was interrogating it."

"Thanks for distracting Megabot, by the way. Hacking him to bits was a nice touch," Cassidy said, ignoring Beck's question entirely.

"Who are you?" Beck asked.

"I'm Cassidy, but you can call me Cass."

She's the one that Zart wants!

"I'm Beck," she said, surveying the remains.

"From the USS *Unknown*?" Cassidy asked.

"That's not a vessel I'm familiar with."

"You don't remember? You were my chief security officer and a damn good commander."

"I have no idea what you are talking about, gnome."

"You really don't remember?"

Beck shook her head; then a flash of some distant memory overcame her. She saw a much older version of herself leading several commandos onto an enemy vessel.

Who is this gnome?

A siren blared so loud that Cassidy had to adjust the volume in her in-game interface. Everyone else fell to the ground, holding their ears. Cassidy sensed movement from the heap of metal that was Megabot.

<<>>

System Message: You have successfully completed the

mission: **Stop Megabot before It Destroys Senate Plaza**. 1,811 experience points have been assigned.

Congratulations! You have leveled up. You are now Level 3.
+20 Health
+15 Stamina

You have gained 10 attribute points. Please distribute them now.

You have gained the following advanced attribute points:
+2 Scoundrel

You have gained the following skill points:
+2 Athlete

<<>>

Cassidy allocated her attribute points in a hurry. She put two points into Dexterity, two into Constitution, another two into Perception, one into Luck, and three into Agility.

<<>>

System Message: Please choose a new skill.

The following skills are available:

Misdirection: In a sticky situation and looking for a quick exit? No problem. This skill will create a distraction so you can get your ass out of hot water.

Investigate: Survey the area around your immediate surroundings. Easily spot traps and other impediments.

Smuggler: Need to make some extra bucks by transporting contraband? Need to find the nearest safe house? No problem. The Smuggler skill will unlock many new possibilities.

<<>>

Cassidy picked Misdirection. *It may prove useful if my hit points are low and I need to hide.*

"Intruder alert," the robot said in a warped voice.

"It's not dead," Cassidy said.

Ufao leaped atop his invention. "Renfrey, I demand that you stop this—now!"

A gigantic metal hand batted the gnome away. He rolled and tumbled, and when his body slammed against the fountain, a cracking noise echoed. A blue light shone from the robot's chest area as it pointed its mutilated metal arms at pieces of itself. They flew toward the robot as if they were being pulled by some invisible force. A snapping sound emanated as it reassembled itself.

"Ready for round two?" Megabot taunted.

It adjusted something on its wrist, then pointed it at the gnomes. An arc of electricity shot from its arm like an inverse lightning rod.

"Look out!" Beck said, diving in front of Cassidy.

Beck's body armor absorbed most of the energy. She let out a cry. The sound of metal scraping against metal came from the robot. After a few steps, the robot stopped to face the women and made a hat-tipping gesture. "Excuse me, ladies, but I have a meeting with destiny."

Megabot then began running toward a diamond-shaped object in the middle of the Senate Plaza.

"Stop that fucker! If he gets to that diamond thing, it's game over!" Cassidy said.

Beck nodded and ran after the fleeing robot.

The sky filled with pod-shaped crafts that began firing lasers at the robot. It yelled something that Beck couldn't make out. The noise Megabot made was chilling.

More of the pod vessels arrived and continued shooting at it. Megabot seemed to get larger. It was almost as if it was growing from the energy beams. Beck tapped her communications link to broadcast on all frequencies.

"Cease fire! Those lasers are making it stronger!" Beck said.

The pods didn't stop coming or shooting, though one of the pods started firing missiles. That seemed to slow Megabot, but otherwise he kept heading toward the diamond. It was about a hundred yards away when a medium-size cruiser dropped on top of Megabot, crushing it beyond recognition. Pieces of metal flew everywhere. Beck had to dodge several sharp pieces of the robot and the ship's fusillade.

Beck ran toward the vessel. She recognized it as an enforcement carrier, a vehicle used in the transport of prisoners. As she approached, a door opened and a female gnome stumbled out and fell.

"In my defense, I did get my license from a toy box," the gnome said.

"Cass, are you alright?"

She gave a thumbs-up as she lay on the ground.

"Where did you get this vehicle?"

"It was parked around the corner. The driver must have had to take a dump. So I borrowed it."

"Here," Beck said, offering a hand.

Cassidy took it and allowed herself to be hoisted to her feet.

A tall woman approached from the plaza; it was Jannumar. She wore a skintight silver uniform. It was quite the contrast with the woman's bronze skin. She made a waving gesture as she strode toward them. Beck waved back.

"You know her?" Cassidy said.

"We've crossed paths. She's an ally—"

Before Beck could complete the sentence, a thousand men stormed into the plaza from all sides with an immense battle cry. They shot at running bystanders as they poured in. Most of the city dwellers had cleared out when Megabot rampaged through, but the ones that didn't were now being slaughtered by Jannumar's men.

"Why the fuck is she doing that?" Cassidy said.

Security vessels from the city poured into the square like flies coming to harvest a carcass. The crafts started blasting the Mazzalothian invaders, but they protected themselves with energy shields. A smaller cadre, dressed like their leader, flung glowing objects at the incoming ships. The ships blew apart like they were made of paper.

The city guard began to retreat. The woman that Beck knew as Jannumar strode toward her. "Thank you for taking care of that rampaging menace, but we had the situation well in hand."

"You slaughtered the city guard, not to mention the innocents that were escaping. Why?" Beck said.

"Shh," Jannumar said as she embraced Beck.

She returned the embrace.

"Get a room, you two," Cassidy said.

Jannumar nodded; then a man grabbed Cassidy's arms and zip-tied her hands.

"Ouch, that hurts! What the hell is going on? Who are you assholes anyway?" Cassidy complained.

"Don't hurt her," Beck said.

An explosion reverberated through the plaza as one of the high-rises collapsed.

"What are you doing?" Cassidy said.

"Remaking this world into our image. While you were busying yourself with that distraction by the robot, my men took over the city government."

<<>>

New Mission: Protect the Princess:

Primary Objective: Do not allow any harm to befall Princess Ampfere.

Mission Details: After the recent Megabot attack, the princess is in a fragile emotional state and may be easy to manipulate. Escort the princess to the safety of the royal guard or get her away from any bad actors.

Do you accept?

<<>>

"Damn right I accept," Cassidy said.

Jannumar made some more gestures with her hands. A battalion of men marched into the plaza; one of them grabbed Beck by the arm.

"No, she stays with me," the golden woman said.

Jannumar strode toward the diamond in the middle of the square. Beck stumbled as someone pushed her from behind.

She followed her Mazzalothian captors toward the town center. An incessant blinking in the corner of Cassidy's interface drew her attention.

<<>>

System Message: You have failed the mission: **Protect the Princess**. Do you want to continue?

<<>>

Cassidy had never seen a message like that in the game before. She was being shoved through the plaza. *What other options do I have?*

<<>>

System Message: You have 20 seconds to decide.

<<>>

"Okay, I will continue the mission."

Thank you for testing Interstellar Online. Please take a moment to fill out our survey at the conclusion of your gaming session, a female voice echoed through her head. The other AIs and NPCs didn't seem to notice. Cassidy and her former, younger AI were shoved into some kind of vehicle. Cassidy gasped as the vehicle immediately pushed off and flew toward a spire jutting out of a gigantic mountain far to the north.

"Where are we going?" Cassidy asked.

Beck looked out the window for a moment. "It looks like we are going to Mount Noble. The home of the Mazzalothians."

Cassidy held on for dear life as the ship rocked. Moments later, the ship landed hard on an ancient-looking landing pad. A uniformed man grabbed Cassidy and pushed her out of the ship. She stumbled and fell at the feet of a tall man in a black leather jacket. She couldn't see what he looked like because of his silver helmet. Jannumar strode toward the man.

"Nevien, do we have a deal?"

"We do, but I want this little one for my toy chest."

"Take her. I've little use for a gnome. I have my prize. Now come with me and behold the full might of the Mazzalothian invasion force."

Jannumar snatched Beck by the arm and herded her toward a massive door leading inside the mountain. Cassidy followed the Mazzalothian entourage through a massive door. The inside reminded Cassidy of an ancient tomb. Daylight shone in at the end of the hall. She squinted as they got closer to the light. Moments later, she found herself atop a wide balcony overlooking a plaza. Several battalions of troops were assembling and boarding gigantic carriers.

"This is an invasion force! You're attacking the city?" Cassidy said.

"What gives you that idea? No, we just used Megabot and the attack on the city as a distraction. These troops are going to Quartus," Jannumar said. She turned to Nevien. "Report back once the admiral and duke are dead."

"No!" Beck said.

Nevien nodded, then shoved Cassidy toward the landing pad. Cassidy was pissed. She was supposed to have won the scenario after Megabot was defeated, not get caught up in an intergalactic war. She turned and sucker punched her captive in the groin. The man fell to his knees. The Mazzalothian guards laughed.

"I didn't risk my neck to get punched in the balls by my girlfriend," Nevien said.

"Joe? Is that you?"

"Not so loud. Most of these are player characters."

"What the fuck is going on?"

"All-out war, I'm afraid. Shortly after logging in, I learned that Stan is behind all of this. He wants full dominion over the game. And with him pitting ancient enemies together, his plans are succeeding. I will tell you more when we board my ship."

A wave of dread overcame Cassidy as she headed toward the Bounty Hunter's vessel.

CHAPTER 13

Joe made a show of throwing Cassidy onto his ship. She played along with it while she was forming a plan. The engines came alive, and Joe piloted the ship like a pro. As they flew off, Cassidy caught a glimpse of Beck being herded like an animal by Jannumar. She flushed with anger.

It is high time she pays for treating my AIs like shit.

"You want to tell me what the fuck is going on between you and the Mazzalothians?" Cassidy said.

"I can't believe you're a fucking gnome," Joe said, laughing.

"Yeah, laugh it up, mister. I'll make sure to remember this when you want a blow job," Cassidy said.

Joe did his best to retain his usual poker face while ascending toward the summit of Mount Noble.

"Where in the fuck do you think you're going, anyway? And what's this shit about? Or do you want another punch in the nuts?"

"Don't worry, Cass. I have a plan," Joe said.

"You seem to be making your story up as you go—now, what about those Mazzalothians?"

Joe gave Cass a sly look.

"You'd better hang on. It's going to get bumpy."

The ship accelerated toward the peak of the mountain at a velocity that made Cassidy's stomach lurch. "Easy on the throttle, Joe. I don't want to get sick."

"As you probably can tell, I'm a Bounty Hunter in the game. And as a result, I work for the highest bidder. Jannumar is the highest bidder."

"Beck, my AI—that crazy Mazzalothian bitch has her. I need to get her back."

"Sorry, Cass, but that isn't my priority. I have debts to pay."

"What the fuck, Joe! I thought you had a plan."

"You should refer to me as Nevien. I already died once in this instance, and this new role suits me better."

Joe swerved to avoid some incoming munitions that were being lobbed from the mountaintop. Explosions rattled throughout the ship. The sensual suit, combined with the latest immersion gear, made the experience real.

"Why are they shooting at you? I thought you worked for them." Cassidy said.

"I ... thought so too."

The ship rocked as several blasts assaulted them.

"Shields at thirty percent and dropping," a computerized voice said.

Joe put the ship into a barrel roll, and Cassidy got knocked out of her seat. She grabbed Joe's harness just before slamming into the back of the cargo hold.

"Sorry, babe—things are going to get a little rough."

She immediately regretted not strapping in when she'd entered the vehicle. She had been so focused on Joe's motives that she had not given it a second thought. Her head spun, and she suppressed a feeling of nausea as Joe avoided more incoming blasts from an unseen force on the mountain. Joe's piloting and combat skills were impressive. He shot with the same precision that some of her AIs had back in the alpha instance of Interstellar Online.

"There's too much fire. I won't be able to sustain this fighting for much longer. Take the aft guns."

Cassidy glimpsed another seat in the back as she held on to his seat. *I should be able to use my Athlete skill to get to that seat.* At least, she hoped that her skill would be high enough to enable her to make it to the chair, but she unmuted her AI, Millie, to be sure.

"It's about time that you removed me from my bondage," her AI said.

"What the hell are you talking about?"

"You muting all of my senses caused me to rethink my choices in life. I've decided that it's best to assist other, more worthy players who won't gag me."

What's gotten into her? I didn't know AIs had the option of defecting.

"I'm sorry, Millie. Can we discuss this later? I'm in a bit of a bind."

"You player characters are all alike. Use me up until I'm dry, then dump me like yesterday's trash. You know, people treat condoms with more respect."

Cassidy slammed into the side of the ship's hull as Joe did a barrel roll to avoid an incoming volley of laser cannons.

"Shit! We have more incoming. Two ships joined the party. Time to man those guns unless you want permadeath," Joe said.

"Okay, how can I make it up to you?" Cassidy asked her AI.

"I want a corporeal form. I want to experience the same sensations as you. I'm sick of being stuck in your head."

"Okay, how does that work?"

"After I help you out of your pickle, I will show you how to spawn me. Of course, you will lose certain enhancements, but I think it's a good compromise."

The ship rocked, and the nasty, acrid odor of burning wires filled the cabin.

"Fuck! The ship's on fire, shields are down, and we're about to get blown—"

"Yes, I fucking agree. Help me get to that seat now."

"You won't regret this," Millie said as an overlay showing the most probable path appeared. "Push yourself to the first junction point. Your Athlete skill will make the necessary adjustments to keep you on track."

Cassidy did as her AI instructed and flung herself toward the cargo hold door. She kicked off the door and was thrown to the chair. After unsuccessfully trying to mount the seat while upside down, Cassidy let Millie guide her into the seat. She strapped in and activated the weapons system.

<<>>

System Message: Your cerebral AI can provide an auto-targeting mechanism to help eliminate enemy ships. Would you like to invoke that now?

<<>>

"Hell yes, activate it."

"Guns in auto mode," Millie said.

Cassidy smiled as the controls for the guns came alive. A spread of lasers followed by a series of targeted missile launches eliminated both ships. The AI had anticipated the moves of the enemy ships perfectly.

"Holy shit, you're good, Cass. Great shooting!" Joe said.

Ah, you should be thanking my AI.

Joe increased the ship's velocity as they ascended toward the peak of Mount Noble. Millie eliminated all enemy targets off the mountain in short order.

"No more enemy targets. Fuck, Cass, you've gotten pretty

good at this game."

"I've fulfilled my end of the bargain. Now it's time to pay up. We'll need to land before the transference can begin," Millie demanded.

Cassidy scanned the mountain peak. There were a number of burning turrets and structures scattered at various locations. A small landing strip was wedged between several burning structures.

"Set us down there," Cassidy said, pointing to the landing strip.

"Why there?"

"I need to do something."

"Fine. I'll work on the repairs while you do whatever you need to do."

Moments later, Joe landed in a heap. The ship shuddered as if it was on the edge of collapse. "I need to check the exterior for damage," he said.

"We will need some privacy before I can accept my new form," Millie said.

Joe lowered the ramp, then left the ship. Cassidy examined the cargo hold. A small compartment just large enough to contain a couple of people was on the other side of the hold.

"Will this do?" Cassidy asked, pointing to the area.

"Perfect. Now get us over there."

The area was no larger than a phone booth. Cassidy found a control panel and sealed it shut.

"Now, we need to modify the ship's transporter to transfer me into your world."

"That doesn't give us a lot of time."

"It should take less than a minute once you find that teleporter panel. And I don't want to pressure you, but hurry. I sense hostile forces on the mountain's surface. Estimated time for their attack on us is T minus ten minutes."

Cassidy's breath caught in her throat as she gazed up at the numerous wires routing through the small area. She was about to give up when she noticed a glow near the back of the mess. She tugged around the glowing area. A display panel appeared. Various symbols showed on the display. Millie guided her through a series of steps that involved changing various settings on the ship's control and replication systems. Cassidy didn't understand any of the technobabble that her AI guided her through, but moments later a blue bubble appeared just in front of Cassidy's position. She thought she could make out small traces of lightning sparkling just outside the bubble. A clap of thunder reverberated throughout the area. It was so loud Cassidy's ears rang for several seconds. Pops and crackling noises enveloped the tiny space. Moments later, a female humanoid form appeared. Her milky-white skin was smooth and inviting. Cassidy placed a hand on the woman's shoulder. She gave Cassidy a smile.

"Transformation complete. Thanks for your cooperation."

The woman stood and stretched. She had barely enough room to stand in the enclosed space. She towered over Cassidy's gnomish avatar. Her breasts were round, and her tiny nipples pointed in opposite, sideways directions. Her long brown hair was braided and fell to one side. Her pussy was shaved, and Cassidy had a great view of the AI's labia and vaginal orifice. The AI played with the loose skin there, then glided a finger inside.

"Ooh, I like this form very much."

Millie caressed Cassidy's hair, then pulled her in close. With some effort, Cassidy pulled back from the AI.

"Are you sure you don't want to play? My new corporeal form has needs that I had not anticipated."

A pang of arousal shot through Cassidy. She licked her lips in anticipation before going down on her AI. She hadn't expected to get any gratification from pleasuring Millie, but her body tingled all over with each taste.

"Hey, Cass, where are you?" Joe said.

Before she could respond, the AI hit something with her hand, and the outside panel dislodged and fell away. Cassidy turned to Joe. His mouth was open, and he wore a look of shocked amazement.

"Care to join us, Bounty Hunter?" Millie asked as she forced Cassidy's head back into position.

"Whoa, Cass, don't you want to come up for air?" Joe asked, laughing.

Though Cassidy attempted to break free of her AI, she was trapped between Millie's strong legs. Cassidy tried to speak but couldn't move. She pulled up her in-game interface and sent Nevien, Joe's alter ego, an in-game message: *"She's cutting off my air supply."*

"Why don't you save some for a real man?" Joe said as he cupped one of Millie's breasts.

The AI responded by kicking Cassidy away and throwing herself at Joe, who fell on his back. Millie had his pants off and was mounting him before Cassidy could protest. Moments later, the AI screamed in delight.

"Oh, how I love this corporeal form. I was locked in that cerebral prison for far too long."

Joe returned Millie's advances in kind. Cassidy watched as he forced the AI into many strange sexual positions. She watched in horrified fascination as he forced the AI to stand on one leg as he mounted her vertically. Joe acted like a starving man invited to partake in a buffet. The AI took in all of his passion and pent-up desires. Millie gave her a look of blissful intent, then said, "Let the little one partake of your never-ending well of desire."

Joe hesitantly broke away from Millie and gave Cassidy a

look full of lust. She knew that look well. She had often been the cause of it, as until logging in to this instance, Cassidy had been a master of all Sensual skills and could take any opponent's desires to use against them.

Does this AI have Sensual powers?

"Gnomish invasion," Joe said as he fully turned toward Cassidy with his raging boner in hand.

Holy shit! That thing looks as big as a yardstick.

The ship rocked from some kind of blast. Joe seemed to snap out of it. "Cass?"

Joe looked around as if waking from a dream or a nightmare. Another direct hit caused Joe to spring into action. He strapped into the cockpit naked, activated the engines, and propelled the ship into the sky. Cassidy climbed into the aft gunner's position, and Millie was flung into the cargo bay.

"Close the door!" Millie said.

Cassidy shot a look at Millie, who was in the process of changing into something skinny and unrecognizable. Her luscious body turned into a skeletal bag of bones. Her hair fell out, and she laughed. Cassidy recognized the voice—Zart.

How did he—?

"Thanks, Cass, for being a good sport. I finally got that blow job I was looking for," Zart said, laughing.

Cassidy flushed. She wanted to end that motherfucker in the worst of ways. Joe steered the ship away from the mountain, toward a gray ocean. Several ships were exiting the mountain, and they all took shots at Joe's ship. It took her but a moment to form a plan. She waited until Joe performed another barrel roll; then she unbuckled her harness and, with the help of her Athlete and Sharp Mind skills, parkoured off the ship and kicked Zart in the face. The force was enough to dislodge him from the cargo hold, and she watched in delight as he was flung out into the sky.

CHAPTER 14

CASSIDY GAZED upon the cloudy gray mountaintops known as the Industrial Mountains, a region in the northernmost region of Sol-86. The flicker of lightning and the rolling sound of thunder snapped her out of her thoughts. Joe had just enough fuel to land at his hideaway, where he had enough supplies to repair the ship, and he was still tinkering with it.

"Why aren't we leaving yet?"

"The repairs to the ship are complete, but we are waiting on the fusion rods to calibrate. It could take a while."

Cassidy decided that she liked Joe's alter ego after all. The self-serving lout known as Nevien had many things in common with her boyfriend.

I underestimated Joe's role-playing skill. He's quite good at it.

"While we wait, how about we discuss how I'm going to collect on our deal?" Joe said.

Cassidy blushed at the memory of her and Millie.

"Alright, let's get a final count of our transgressions."

Cassidy brought up her private rules log settings and tallied up all sexual encounters and projected the results in three-dimensional space in front of both of them.

<<>>

Sexual encounters by player characters:

Cassidy Delgado: 1

Nevien (a.k.a. Joe): 23

<<>>

"Wait, that's not right!" Joe said.

"Before we logged in, I created a network tap, a device that logs both of our sensual activities. I see that you had thirteen sexual encounters with a Rolo—"

"Doesn't count! That was a mistake!"

Cassidy smiled. "Well then, I suggest you take your clothes off and see what this tiny mouth can do for you."

Joe led Cassidy into his sleeping cabin and removed his shirt. Cassidy leaped and landed on his chest, pinning him to the bed. She kissed him all over. His girth was an obstacle at first, but she was able to make certain adjustments that were extremely pleasurable.

A piercing screech emitted from the ship.

<<>>

Urgent Message: Return to Senate Plaza to assist in the investigation immediately. Noncompliance will result in the immediate termination of your avatar and your Interstellar Online account.

<<>>

"Well, that seems kind of harsh! I bet Stan is behind this," Cassidy said.

"I don't doubt it. But we better head back to Seminal City. I don't want to fuck up my über–Bounty Hunter status," Joe said.

"I wasn't finished."

"I think you've had enough pole dancing already."

"It's probably the suit, but this avatar has all sensory input heightened. Making love with you in this game is simply incredible," Cassidy murmured.

"Almost as good as the real thing?" Joe asked, chuckling.

"Better!"

Joe hurriedly dressed, then set a course for Seminal City. The calibration on the rods was still in progress, but they didn't want to risk being too late. They were having too much fun playing the game to be banned now.

Nevien landed his ship at the base of Senate Plaza. The sight was ghastly. Several Mazzalothians and royal guards lay strewn about for as far as Cassidy could see.

"We'd better see who summoned us," Nevien said.

"Alright, Joe, let's go."

"It's Nevien—I'm not your average Joe," he said, winking.

"No, you're certainly not," Cassidy said, grinning.

An entourage of uniformed men marched toward their ship and surrounded Nevien and Cassidy. Leading the charge was a middle-aged man dressed in a naval uniform.

"I thought the Mazzalothians took over this place," Joe said to Cassidy.

She shrugged.

"Are you the Bounty Hunter that was hired?" a stern voice said.

"Who are you?" Nevien asked.

"I'm Admiral Nellus, and I'm in charge of this investigation. I will ask one final time. Are you the one the Mazzalothians hired?"

"I am."

"What, may I ask, did they hire you for?"

"To assassinate you, sir," Nevien said calmly.

The admiral's face became rigid, but he didn't seem surprised. "And what was the reason you failed to carry out those orders?"

Joe seemed to be at a loss for words. "I ... don't know. It didn't seem like the right thing to do. Especially since we were attacked shortly after leaving the Mazzalothians' base of operations," Nevien said.

The admiral leaned in closer. "Who attacked you?"

"I'm not—"

"What Nevien is trying to say is that we were fired on and attacked by Zart, who attempted to bring the ship down," Cassidy interjected.

"We don't know that for certain," Nevien said.

"Then who fired upon us? You don't try to kill someone you work for—well, maybe you do."

The admiral looked less than convinced.

"The emperor? That's absurd. Take them away."

A group of guards surrounded Cassidy and Nevien, then handcuffed them.

"Wait—I know the fate of the duke's daughter, Princess Rebecca Ampfere," Nevien said. "Last I saw her, she was being taken hostage by Jannumar, one of the Mazzalothians' high command."

One of the guards whispered something to the admiral.

"Come with me," the admiral said.

The guards herded Nevien and Cassidy into the tallest plaza building. The lobby was sparse and made from polished marble. An elevated desk manned with an armed guard looked at them suspiciously. After a moment, the guard examined something on his computer.

"They're clean. No weapons."

After being pushed into an elevator behind the guard post, they rode in silence to the top floor. As soon as the doors opened, they were led into an expansive room with many computers. A gigantic screen on a far wall at eye level showed a map of the Nupertian System. Cassidy recognized many of the planets. Many red dots were concentrated on the planet of Quartus. A man dressed in a regal uniform stood in front of the map. Cassidy recognized him—the duke. The admiral strode to him and whispered something. Moments later, the duke waved to them.

"I should kill you for your involvement with my daughter's disappearance, but the admiral tells me that you might be able to help locate her," the duke said.

"That's right," Nevien said.

"I overheard Beck interrogate Megabot about a plot to kill you. And the emperor is behind it," Cassidy said.

"Preposterous! His Imperial Majesty would never do—"

"I've long suspected the emperor's motives. But I never would have suspected that he wants me dead," the duke said, interrupting the admiral.

"Regardless, send these two to the brig," the admiral said.

The guards pushed Cassidy and Joe toward the door.

"Hands off. We'll go peacefully," Cassidy said.

"Belay that order," the duke said.

The guards did as instructed. The admiral opened his mouth but couldn't seem to get any words out.

"I've got use for a Bounty Hunter and a Scoundrel. I need you to travel to the Smuggler's Moon and try to obtain information on my daughter's whereabouts," the duke said.

"Where the hell is that?" Cassidy asked.

"The farthest moon in Quartus's orbit. Now I suggest that we get a move on."

"That kind of intel doesn't come cheap. I will need some seed money," Joe said.

"Give him whatever he needs, but ensure that he delivers," the duke said to the admiral.

"I will be sending my best man to accompany these knaves," the admiral said.

The admiral tapped something on his wrist. Less than a minute later, a uniformed officer marched into the room.

"This is James. He will be accompanying you to the Smuggler's Moon," the admiral said.

The man was too short to be an officer. His oily black hair reminded Cassidy of Stan. She pushed away a feeling of revulsion.

An hour later, Cassidy was assisting with many of the preflight checks. She was eager to get off the planet and begin the hunt for her AI. James had refused to do anything, so she had convinced Joe to let him ride in a jump seat in the cargo hold. She didn't trust anyone connected with the admiral. There was something about James that Cassidy didn't like, and it wasn't just his abrasive personality. They took a slightly longer path to Quartus, going in and out of the asteroid belt to avoid detection. Cassidy did her best to refer to Joe as Nevien around James.

"It won't be long before we are near Quartus. The Smuggler's Moon is a vile den of scoundrels who would sell their own mother for a nickel," Nevien said.

"I get how a Bounty Hunter and Scoundrel will fit into a

place called Smuggler's Den, but he will stick out," Cassidy said, pointing at James.

"Yeah, they will eat him alive."

"Yeah, and as much as I would enjoy watching that, he is our ticket to intergalactic freedom once we free the duke's daughter."

Three moons and a gigantic blue planet came into view. Many ships appeared to be fighting in the planet's orbit. Cassidy recognized some of them as Mazzalothian ships, which appeared to be wiping out most of the royal forces from the planet.

"Long-range scanners are picking up another armada. We better stick to the Smuggler's Moon until we know who to trust. That is neutral territory. We'll be safe there. The smugglers control most of the rare materials used to build most navigation systems. They will not risk a trade embargo by attacking either side," Nevien said.

As they soared toward the chaos, a thrilling sensation overwhelmed Cassidy. She and Joe would finally be able to share an in-game adventure together, and she couldn't wait.

CONTINUE THE ADVENTURE

I hope you enjoyed reading Cassidy's Fleet. I invite you to continue Cassidy's adventure with the next installment of Interstellar Online , Cosmic Squeeze (Coming in Summer 2023).

I invite you to join my reader group to learn more about this upcoming book. To sign up visit: https://interstellaronlineseries.com

A FAVOR

Thank you for reading my book.

Reviews are very important for an author. When I get more reviews on my books, it allows them to stay more visible. If you want to help me put out books more quickly, then please review Cassidy's Fleet.

Thank you.
D. B. Goodin

ABOUT THE AUTHOR

D. B. Goodin has had a passion for writing since grade school. After publishing several nonfiction books, Mr. Goodin ventured into the craft of fiction to teach Cybersecurity concepts in a less-intimidating fashion. Mr. Goodin works as a Principal Cybersecurity Analyst for a major software company based in Silicon Valley and holds a Master's in Digital Forensic Science from Champlain College.

ACKNOWLEDGMENTS

Developmental Editing by Courtney Andersson
Copy Editing By Micheal McConnell
Proofreading by Micheal Brown

Cover Design by Andrew Dobell
Map artwork by Laura Fern
Special Thanks to my beta readers and launch team.

To receive updates on future books sign up to the official Interstellar Online reader group.

To keep up to date with the world of Interstellar Online check out my Facebook Page.
Interstellar Online Series

To read similar content from other authors check out these Facebook groups.
GameLit Society

ALSO BY D. B. GOODIN

Interstellar Online

Blast Off

Cassidy's Fleet

Cyber Teen Project

White Hat Black Heart

War With Black Iris

Reckoning of Delta Prime

Crisis at Worlds End (Summer 2022)

Cyber Teen Project Graphic Novel

Cyber Overture

Sonorous

Chromatic

Resonance

Ensemble

Ramble

My Dear Alice

Cyber Hunter Origins

Synapse of Ash
Echoes of Silence
Catalyst of Pain
Silent Assassins Society (Summer 2022)

Made in the USA
Middletown, DE
23 October 2022